A CANDLE IN THE DARK

'Did Mr Padgett have a hurrier before?' There was no laughter. The dim face before him seemed to tense. 'Yes.' Joe said nothing else, so Jimmy said, 'What happened to him?'
'Accident.'
'What sort of accident?'
'Something bashed him on the head.' Joe's answers were reluctant.
'Something?'
'Don't ask,' said Joe. He was whispering now.
'What bashed him on the head?' Jimmy almost shouted.
Joe let go one of his shoulders to thrust a hand over his companion's mouth. 'Shhh,' he hissed. 'We're near the bottom now. Don't ask. Just do everything Mr Padgett tells ye.' Jimmy sensed Joe's fear, and it added to his own.

Will Jimmy discover the dangerous secret of Rawdon Pit?

About the author

Robert Swindells was born in Bradford, West Yorkshire in 1939. He left school at fifteen, and subsequently worked as a proof reader on local papers, joined the RAF as a clerk, and on leaving the RAF had a number of jobs, including printing and engineering. In 1969 he entered college to train as a teacher. While there he wrote his first novel, *When Darkness Comes* as a thesis, and this was published by Hodder and Stoughton in 1973. He continued writing and teaching, but gradually writing took over, and in 1980 he became a full-time writer.

A Candle in the Dark

Robert Swindells

Illustrated by Gareth Floyd

KNIGHT BOOKS
Hodder and Stoughton

For Ian Aitken, who knows the reason why

First published by David and Charles Ltd 1974 under the title *A Candle in the Night*

Knight Books edition 1983

Third impression 1991

British Library C.I.P.

Cataloguing in Publication Data is available from the British Library

ISBN 0 340 32098 2

The characters and situations in this book are entirely imaginary and bear no relation to any real person or actual happenings.

Printed and bound in Great Britain for Hodder and Stoughton Children's Books, a division of Hodder and Stoughton Ltd., Mill Road, Dunton Green, Sevenoaks, Kent TN13 2YA. (Editorial Office: 47 Bedford Square, London WC1B 3DP) by Cox & Wyman Ltd., Reading, Berks.

I

IT WAS cold in the yard and his fingers hurt. Picking oakum was painful, as well as monotonous, and this morning's lot had been more tarry than usual. Sitting hunched in the long gallery, picking the tarry rope into shreds, while the master patrolled up and down, back and forth between the skeps with the rod in his hand. Don't look up. Never look up. And don't stop, even for a moment. Ignore the ache in your back from bending, and the ache in your stomach from hunger. And if the boy next to you whispers, don't reply, or it will be the rod for the pair of you, and no supper.

Now, the yard. Jimmy screwed up his eyes against the pale sun that seemed to hang just over the high wall. Sixty boys, shuffling into thin, pale lines, in rags. Teeth clenched, faces wan like the sun.

Jimmy got into his place, between John Ogden and Eli who had no second name. He knew by now that it was better to quell the hope that flickered inside him. Sixty boys. Why should it be his turn? He had never been chosen. Too thin. Tall, but stringy. Outgrown his strength, they said. So Jimmy would watch as the massive gates creaked open, and the chosen boys walked away with their new masters. They never looked back when they went. The gates would close behind them, and there would be only the footfalls, hurrying away beyond the wall. There were two ways of getting out of the Union Workhouse. That was one of them.

Now the gates stood open and the boys shuffled expectantly. Nobody came in. Four old paupers came out of the men's ward, staggering under the weight of the long pale box that they carried. They followed a warden across the yard and out through the gate, which promptly slammed shut again. That was the other way out. Jimmy shuddered and rubbed his hands together for warmth.

'Stand still there!' The line of boys stiffened, and Jimmy pushed his hands down by his sides. The master strode across the yard and stood before them. He had a gentleman with him. Jimmy recognised him as one of the guardians; one of the wealthy townsmen who were responsible for administering the workhouse. The gentleman always came when apprentices were being chosen. He would tell the boys how fortunate were the ones selected to learn a trade and be independent. He always gave a sovereign to each of the tradesmen who took a boy away; to buy clothes and shoes for his new apprentice. Jimmy felt the flickering again. New clothes! Shoes! A life outside the workhouse, and wages, too! The flickering became a fierce yearning in spite of his efforts to suppress it. He heard hardly anything of what the gentleman said.

At last the gates opened again and a number of men walked in. They were covered with grime, so that it was difficult to tell where black skin ended and black clothing began. Colliers. Jimmy had heard stories about the pits. But nothing could be worse than the workhouse. He straightened up and tried to look strong. The colliers spoke briefly with the master, then came along the rows inspecting the boys: pulling them about, squeezing their arms and poking black fingers into protruding ribs. Soon, several boys were standing out near the master, smirking at the others. Four colliers had looked Jimmy over and had passed on. 'It's the same again,' he told himself bitterly. A giant of a man stopped in front of him.

'Strong, are ye?'

Jimmy started. 'Y-yes, sir,' he stammered.

'Don't look it!' The man looked back along the row. 'But there's worse. A sight worse!' he growled. 'All right, get out in front!'

Jimmy's head spun. He was chosen! Out in front, he received the slaps and prods of the other chosen, and the envious stares of those left behind. He felt dazed, so that he hardly knew what was going on. He heard the big collier asking the master, 'How old is he?' and the master saying, 'We don't know; found wandering. Old enough, I'd say.' (This with a short humourless laugh.)

'Eight years bed and vittles and nary a hand's turn of work!'

Then he was following the others out through the gates. His new master strode in front of him, one black hand clutching his sovereign. New clothes! Jimmy

trotted at the big man's heels, breathless with anticipation. The collier turned down a side-street. Jimmy glanced back once at the grim wall behind him, and followed. The others had gone off in various directions, and he was alone with his master.

'Thank you, sir,' he said to the massive back.

'Eh?' The collier glanced over his shoulder. 'Shut yer mouth.' And he strode on. Undaunted, Jimmy trotted along behind, full of his good fortune. The way became more narrow, and the alley was littered with garbage. There was an unpleasant smell: worse even than the thin smell of the workhouse.

Presently they came to a building with a painted sign. Jimmy could not read the words on it, but it had a picture of a gentleman in a fine blue coat and shining boots. The collier stopped. 'Is this the place where you will buy me new clothes?' cried Jimmy. The big man stared at him as though puzzled; then he threw back his head and roared with laughter.

'Oh aye!' he spluttered. 'Aye, this is where yer sovereign gets spent!' And he went off into fresh roars of mirth. It was Jimmy's turn to look puzzled. Had he said something funny?

There was a lot of laughter inside the building, too, and while the collier was still shaking, a man came out, slapped him on the back with a grimy paw, and roared: 'Now then, Charlie! What's this? Another hurrier to bash on the head?' Then he tottered away unsteadily along the alley. The collier stopped laughing and gazed after the retreating figure.

'Watch your mouth, Tom Fawcett,' he muttered thickly. They both watched until Tom Fawcett staggered out of sight, then the big man turned on Jimmy. 'Don't ye pay no heed to what *he* says, ye hear?' he hissed. His grip hurt the boy's shoulder. 'No, sir!' gasped Jimmy.

'Wait 'ere.' And he went up the steps and through the door from which Tom Fawcett had emerged. Jimmy gazed at the door for a moment, then sat down on the top step. He was hungry and it was getting colder. He wrapped his arms around his stomach and sat watching the shadows lengthen in the alley. The words of Tom Fawcett kept repeating in his head. Another hurrier to bash on the head. The man had been referring to him. What was a hurrier? And why were they bashed on the head?

After a long time, he found himself thinking about the gruel they would be eating now in the long gallery, and his head sank on to his bony knees, and he cried softly in the dusk.

2

'DON'T STAND there dithering, man; show him in!' Hugh Rawdon propped the fowling-piece against the desk and turned toward the door. Damn! Why was it that whenever he was about to exercise the dogs, or to try for a trout, somebody called on business? At this time of day, too. He glanced through the window. Dusk, with just sufficient light to shoot by if a pheasant got up. In twenty minutes it would be dark.

His scowling face brightened a little when his visitor was ushered through the door. 'Ah, Cartwright!' He waited, until the servant had left, closing the door behind him. Then he spoke softly. 'What news from London, man?'

Cartwright spoke, smirking. 'I reckon they bought it, sir: most of 'em, any road. It's the talk of every tavern in the City, from what I could 'ear.'

Rawdon smiled. 'Splendid. Then Mr Joseph Croft will hardly dare to show his face there!' He paced the room, slamming a fist into his palm and muttering, half to himself. 'Now perhaps I shall have less of his damned interference!' He turned to his informant. 'You have done well, you and the others. Tell them they'll be paid as promised. I want you to take a note to the master at the workhouse for me.' He pulled a bellcord. 'Remain here: Wilkins will bring you some refreshment.' The manservant appeared and Rawdon left the room.

He blew gently on the note to dry the ink, and read it through:

Dear Mr White,

Further to our conversation of a week ago: I have good reason for believing that we shall have no further trouble from our mutual friend. Rest easy, therefore, and let the excellent arrangement between yourself and my colliers stand.

He folded and sealed the note, smiling faintly, and rose from the escritoire. Twilight lingered still between the trees. Another ten minutes, perhaps. Time enough, if he hurried.

3

THE CLATTER of clogs began before dawn. On the floor by the big copper, Jimmy stirred, and opened his eyes. It was cold. The room was quite dark still. He pulled the thin blanket up over his shoulders and shivered. Across the room, he could make out the small square of the window and the stars beyond. More footsteps, and muffled voices, passing. Jimmy shivered again. The cold flags struck their chill into his thin body. He was hungry. Upstairs, somebody was moving. Jimmy sat up, stiffly. The window was paler now and he could see the table in the middle of the floor, and the two chairs.

It had been late when the collier had emerged from the tavern, and he had awakened the boy with a kick. Jimmy had followed his master in a daze of fatigue down alleys and along dim, gaslit streets between rows of cramped, grimy cottages until they came, at last, to the home of Charlie Padgett. Jimmy had a dim recollection of a peeling door that had opened to spill lamplight on the greasy cobbles. Inside, it had been warmer. A few coals glowed under the copper. A thin woman was there, her face seeming, to Jimmy's weary eyes, to hover like a crinkly white mask over the oil lamp. The mask had fired one question at him in a thin, whiny voice. 'What do they call ye, then?' and he had answered flatly, 'Jimmy Booth.' There had been a bowl of porridge, thicker than workhouse gruel, and a chunk of bread. Then his corner by the copper, and the blanket, thinner than a workhouse blanket. He had drifted to sleep while the two strangers ate and muttered at the table and he had been far away when the pale lamp went out and they went away without a glance in his direction.

Somebody was coughing on the stairs, coming down. Jimmy got to his feet. There was a curtain over the doorway to the stairs, and candlelight flickered behind it. The curtain moved aside and Mrs Padgett came through.

'Light the lamp, then,' she whined. 'Just got up, I suppose?'

Jimmy, who felt as though he had only been in bed for an hour, said, 'Yes, Ma'am.'

'Aye, well, we didn't take you in out of charity, so you needn't think it.' She thrust the candle at him. 'Light it with this.' While he lit the lamp, Mrs Padgett shuffled over to the copper and began to rake out the ashes from underneath, muttering as she did so. When the lamp was lit, he set the candle down on the table. The woman pointed to it. 'Blow it out, then—a penny a dozen, they cost.' Jimmy blew out the candle.

Upstairs, Charlie Padgett was grunting, putting on

his clogs. The woman pushed a bucket toward the boy with her foot. 'Fill this with coals,' she snapped.

Jimmy hurried to pick up the bucket, then hesitated. 'Where, Ma'am?' he asked quietly.

She spun to face him. 'In the cellar, charity boy, where else?' she screeched. Her bony finger pointed to a door beside the curtained stairway. 'Down there!'

'I was never in a house before, ma'am,' said Jimmy. The woman glared.

'Do as I say, and none of your lip!'

Jimmy opened the door and felt his way down the steep stairs in the dark. There was a musty, damp smell. At the bottom he stumbled into a pile of coals. A crack of weak dawn light showed the place in the wall where the coal was shot in from the street. He filled the bucket, picking up the coals with his hands, and turned to climb back up the stairs. The bucket was heavy. He gasped as he lugged his burden upward and the bucket scraped on the steps. When he reached the top Charlie was there, watching him.

'By gaw!' he growled. 'Ye make heavy weather of that, boy. Wait till ye get a corve fastened to ye!' Mrs Padgett laughed unpleasantly.

'A corve?' said Jimmy, setting down the bucket. 'What is a corve, please?'

'A coal-waggon,' grunted Charlie. 'A tram. What ye'll be pulling for yer keep from now on.' And he sat down at the table while his wife lit the fire and began to make porridge in the copper. Jimmy was sent down the yard for water and then told to keep out of the way until the food was ready. He sat on his blanket. The thought of what was to happen today frightened him, but he tried to tell himself that he was glad to be out of the workhouse; although he was no longer sure that this was true. 'I shall have wages,' he thought. Then he remembered the new clothes he should have had, and wondered if his wages would follow his sovereign into the tavern. Presently, a bowl was thrust at him, and he ate the lumpy porridge mechanically, lost in thought. The clogs were still hurrying by outside.

'Come on, you—never mind that!' Charlie was snatching the unfinished food away from him. 'No daydreaming on Charlie Padgett's time!' Jerked from his thoughts, Jimmy scrambled to his feet. 'Here!' Charlie tossed something at him. 'That's yer snap!'

Jimmy caught it. It was a grubby rag with something tied up inside it. 'Snap?' he said wonderingly.

'Food! All ye'll get till tonight,' Charlie told him. 'So hang on to it.' And then they were out of the door and away down the cold street.

The headgear stood silhouetted against the pale dawn. A black straggle of men and boys shuffled toward it. The wheel turned, and stopped, and turned the other way. The line of black men shortened slowly. Jimmy stood beside his silent master and gazed around. There were a number of boys in the line, most of them standing beside men whom Jimmy took to be their masters. A few were bigger than himself, but some looked much younger than the twelve years he believed his own age to be. All of them looked tired and thin. They were black, from their caps to their feet. Most of them were barefooted. Sometimes, one of the boys would yell a greeting to another, but mostly they stood quietly, waiting their turn to go below.

Just in front of Jimmy stood a very small boy. His cap didn't come up to Jimmy's shoulder. He seemed to be alone. He held a partly finished wooden toy in one hand, and a knife in the other. He was whittling away at this toy, which looked like some sort of cart. Once, he glanced round, seeming to start as he saw Charlie Padgett behind him. He turned quickly round again and resumed his whittling. Jimmy studied the smaller boy. He was stooped, like a little old man, and his breeches were patched and ragged. He had on a shirt with small tears in it, through which the skin of his back showed as black as the cotton. Only his hands and face were clean, and these had small blue scars where cuts and scratches had healed with the coal-dust still in them. As he whittled, the child whistled through his teeth, a tuneless sound.

The line shuffled forward, until presently the shaft yawned before them. Jimmy gazed wonderingly at the apparatus of the headgear, and at the dark pit mouth. An old man was operating the winding-gear. This consisted of a great iron wheel with a handle, which turned the creaking roller that spanned the chasm. Around this roller was wound a thick, oily chain. The chain ended in a ring, from which two short chains hung in an inverted 'v' shape, with a thick iron bar between the wide ends. As Jimmy watched, a collier grabbed this bar and pulled it to the rim of the shaft. He gripped the short chains with his hands and sat on the bar. His boy then sat in the collier's lap, facing him, with his own legs either side of his master, and dangling behind. He held to the collier's shoulders as the bar swung out over the shaft and began to descend, swaying a little. Jimmy swallowed hard and plucked at Padgett's sleeve. 'I thought we would go down in a cage,' he said. Padgett laughed brutally.

'Not at Rawdon Pit, we don't. Cage gear costs money. Clatch-irons are cheap, but if it were up to the owner, we wouldn't even have that—we'd *jump* down!'

He laughed again and lapsed into silence. Jimmy watched the chain unwinding and tried to stop his trembling. Too soon, the roller stopped, and the clatch-harness was coming up again. There was only the small boy in front now.

The old man called out from the wheel, 'You! New boy! You go down with the little 'un!'

Jimmy glanced wildly at his master. 'Please—I want to go down with you.'

Charlie Padgett only shrugged. 'Two little 'uns is easier to lower. Get going!' And he leaned out and caught the clatch-iron for them. The very small boy grinned at Jimmy.

'There's nowt to it,' he chirped. 'You sit on, and I'll cross-lap ye.' Gingerly Jimmy sat on the bar. He gripped the chains till his knuckles were white. The child sat on his lap and held his shoulders. 'Let go, Mr Padgett,' he said. 'I'll look after this one.'

'You shut yer mouth, Trapper Joe, or I'll shut it for ye,' growled Padgett.

He let go the harness. Jimmy screwed up his eyes as he felt the chasm beneath. The child was chuckling in his face, quite unmoved. The roller creaked. Darkness washed up over them. Jimmy opened his eyes, but his grip remained like iron. The child's face was inches from his own. 'It's yer first day, isn't it?' he said.

'Yes,' said Jimmy, concentrating on holding on. 'How did the old man know?'

'Yer clothes is clean,' said the other simply. 'Won't be tonight, though. You Mr Padgett's new hurrier?'

'Hurrier?' said Jimmy. 'I don't know. What's a hurrier?'

The small boy laughed shrilly in the blackness. The sound of it echoed eerily. 'A boy what hurries with the corves,' he said.

Jimmy nodded, thinking about not slipping off the bar. 'He said something about corves.'

This started the child laughing again. 'He said something about corves,' he echoed, between whoops of laughter. 'My, how green we are!'

Jimmy spoke loudly, to stop the laughing. 'Why are you called Trapper Joe?'

'Because I'm called Joe and I'm a trapper.'

Jimmy sensed another whoop coming and said quickly, 'Did Mr Padgett have a hurrier before?'

There was no laughter. The dim face before him seemed to tense. 'Yes.'

Jimmy waited as the clatch-iron dropped through the darkness. The creaking seemed far away now. Water was dripping on to them from somewhere. Joe said nothing else, so Jimmy said, 'What happened to him?'

'Accident.'

'What sort of accident?'

'Something bashed him on the head.' Joe's answers were reluctant.

'Something?'

'Don't ask,' said Joe. He was whispering now.

'What bashed him on the head?' Jimmy almost shouted.

Joe let go one of his shoulders to thrust a hand over his companion's mouth. 'Shhh!' he hissed. 'We're near the bottom now. Don't ask. Just do everything Mr Padgett tells ye.' Jimmy sensed Joe's fear, and it added to his own.

They finished their descent in silence and Jimmy found

himself standing up to his ankles in mud. The harness ascended somewhere above their heads. A man stood at the shaft-bottom with a lamp. He held it so that it shone into the boys' faces. 'Get to yer trap, Joe,' he said. Jimmy started. He recognised the voice of Tom Fawcett. 'You're the new lad of Padgett's.' It was a statement. 'You wait here till he comes down.' Fawcett paused, then added, 'And watch yerself, lad!' He went along the tunnel, crouching. The lamp bobbed and flickered, disappearing. Jimmy could hear the gear far above, creaking down with his master. What was it about his master that everybody told him to beware?

Water was dripping into the shaft, and Jimmy was already half-soaked. He moved into the tunnel. Even he had to crouch a little there, but there was no dripping.

All those who had descended before him seemed to have vanished. Swallowed up. He could not even hear anything, except the distant creaking of the gear, and echoes, too distorted to identify.

Something touched his sleeve, so that he started, crying out sharply. It was Trapper Joe. 'Listen!' the small boy hissed, urgently. 'Stay out of closed road. Padgett'll tell ye. Some of the lads might dare ye to go in, but they'll not have been in themselves! Stay out!'

He turned to go back up the tunnel. Jimmy grabbed at the torn shirt. 'Have *you* been in closed road?' he said softly.

Joe nodded. 'Aye! And owner knows it, and one of these days there'll be another accident down 'ere, and this time it'll be me. Let go now for 'ere comes Padgett!'

Jimmy glanced towards his master's lamp, and when he looked again, Trapper Joe was gone.

4

JOSEPH CROFT smoothed out the letter and read it again. His face was pale, and the hand that held the thick vellum trembled a little as he read. His lips moved soundlessly, forming the words.

There was no mistake: his allies in London had swallowed the rumour. He clenched his hand, screwing the letter for the second time into his palm and throwing it among the breakfast remnants on the table. He pushed back his chair.

'Horace!' The door opened quietly.

'Yes, sir?'

'Make the fire in my study, and set out my writing things. Have the boy ready to take a letter into the town.' The manservant inclined his head, withdrawing. 'And, Horace . . .'

'Sir?'

'I want no interruption.'

Croft rose, moving to stand at the window. The mist was dispersing and the roofs of Rawdon House were visible among the tall oaks. Croft gazed in their direc-

tion until he heard Horace leave the study. 'You scoundrel, Rawdon,' he said softly. 'You unutterable blackguard.' He turned and went swiftly to his study. Normally a mild-mannered man, his anger burned in him now so that he slammed the door and threw himself into the chair behind the leather-topped desk. He reached for a quill and dipped it. His hand was trembling. He paused, breathing deeply, until the quill was steady. Then he addressed a sheet and wrote:

My dear Grey,

I am in receipt of your letter dated the fourth, and am distressed to learn of the credence given in certain quarters to the vile innuendo concerning my brother. As you will know, he was as devoted to our scheme as I am myself and, though his disappearance coincided with the theft of practically all we possessed, I am utterly convinced of his innocence. I believe, in fact, that some tragedy befell him and that the thieves, whoever they are, could shed light upon it were they ever to be apprehended.

That support for my school of industries is being withheld on the grounds that I am the brother of an unprincipled rascal is quite intolerable: I cannot understand how men who have met and spoken with my brother could fail to perceive the depth of his concern for the poor children who toil in our mines.

The rumour that he took our fortune and fled abroad owes its birth, I suspect, to our old friend Hugh Rawdon: the school of industries would deprive him of his little slaves, and it is obviously in his interest to discredit me.

Allow me to assure you once more, dear friend, of my brother's innocence, and to beg you to intercede on our behalf with those who doubt our sincerity.

He paused, scanning the lines he had written. His lips were compressed, bloodless. If he lost the support of his acquaintances in London then he would accomplish nothing. Grey still believed in him: Grey would speak to the others; would win them back, if he could. Mouthing a silent prayer, Joseph Croft signed the letter and reached for the bellcord that would summon the boy.

5

Charlie Padgett ducked into the tunnel and gave his new apprentice a heavy shove. 'Get a move on, will ye? We're late at the face as it is!' Jimmy stumbled forward into the dark, stubbing his toes on the metal rail which ran along the muddy floor. He recovered himself and went slowly forward, his hands out in front of him. The light from Padgett's lamp barely penetrated the darkness: a darkness so palpable that it felt like solid matter. The boy cried out as his head struck something in the roof, and he staggered, clutching at the rough wall for support. Padgett, coming up behind, spat a curse and aimed a kick at Jimmy's shin, so that he cried out again. 'Keep yer feet, yer clumsy brat!' he growled. 'And ger a move on!'

Jimmy put up a blackened hand to rub the sore place on his head. 'It's very low,' he said. 'And narrow.'

Padgett grunted. 'This is the main road. Wait till ye ger in the workings!'

The floor had a slight upward slope, and as they walked, the mud gave way to dry rubble and dust. Jimmy winced as his naked foot came down on to something sharp. The balls of his feet felt raw. 'Don't kick rubble over the rails,' said Padgett. 'Derail a corve and I'll bray ye all round the pit!' Jimmy made no reply, but plunged on. It was becoming hot. He could hear voices, somewhere up ahead. His master's hand gripped his shoulder, halting him. 'We turn here,' he grunted. 'Up the side-gate and through to the other main road. Remember this, for ye'll be hurryin' this way soon.'

A narrower tunnel led off to their left, and they entered it. This time Padgett went first. There was no slope here, and no rails. They went a few paces, then Padgett stopped, holding up his lamp. The light revealed a solid wooden gate, blocking the tunnel. 'Open up, Joe, ye idle whelp!' he cried savagely. 'Every time I come up this gate I catch ye sleeping.'

Jimmy screwed his eyes into the dark. He could see nobody at first, but Padgett swung his lamp and the light spilled into an opening, a hole in the wall. At the back of this hole squatted Trapper Joe. His hole was not high enough for him to sit up straight and he squatted with his back hunched and his head forward.

'Was not sleepin', Mr Padgett,' he said in a frightened voice. 'Was lookin' t'other way.'

'One day ye'll be lookin' t'other way when something hits ye!' growled Padgett. 'Come on—get this thing out of my way!' Joe hauled on the gate, which slid heavily into the hole until its end pinned him to the back wall, and the way was clear. Padgett went through with the lamp and the hole was plunged into utter darkness. As Jimmy made to follow his master, Joe's voice came out of the gloom.

'This is trappin', master Jimmy. How d'ye like it?'

'It...it's very dark,' said Jimmy, 'and you must be

lonely here by yourself. Don't they let you have a candle?'

A chuckle, eerily disembodied. 'No candle: candles cost money.' Jimmy stumbled on, following the lamp.

They came out into the other main road. There were rails again. As they came out of the side-gate a tram was coming along the rails. It was piled high with coal and there was a candle stuck on the front of it with a lump of mud. When it reached the side-gate, the boy who was pushing it came round to the front and eased it off the rails; first the front wheels, then the back. He was panting, and his near-naked body glistened with black sweat. He paid no attention to the watchers, but got behind his corve again and, pushing with hands and head, disappeared into the side-gate. 'Don't stand there gawping!' shouted Padgett. 'That's one corve off already, and we haven't started yet!' They went on. Jimmy's back hurt from stooping, and his feet were cut and sore. He felt as though he had been in the pit for hours, though he knew it could only have been minutes. He kept seeing in his head a picture of little Joe, alone in that black hole. He shuddered.

As they went slowly onward, Jimmy saw a number of very low, narrow tunnels leading off into the black wall on his left. He could hear voices, and when he crouched to look into one of the tunnels he saw light gleaming, dully, deep inside. Padgett glanced back and saw the boy's wondering expression.

'Workings,' he grunted. 'Ours is just up ahead.'

After a few more yards Padgett stopped, and Jimmy thought that they must have reached their destination.

Padgett beckoned him forward and pointed to a hole in the glistening black wall. 'This is an abandoned working,' he said. There was menace in his voice. 'Dangerous. The roof-props are cracking and the roof could cave in at any time. Whatever happens, yer never to go into that working. Do ye understand?' His fingers dug into the boy's shoulder, like last night outside the tavern. Jimmy gritted his teeth.

'Yes, sir,' he gasped. 'Trapper Joe told me.'

Padgett glanced at him sharply. 'Told ye? Told ye what?' The grip tightened.

'Not to go in. He said other boys might dare me,' said Jimmy, squirming under the iron fingers.

'Trapper Joe has too much trap!' snarled Padgett. 'I'll not have ye talking to him. And think on: keep out of closed road.'

Presently, they came to Padgett's working. The big man dropped on all-fours and crawled in. Jimmy followed. It was so narrow in the working that Padgett's shoulders scraped the walls as he moved forward, and his cap rasped along the jagged roof.

As he crawled, Jimmy felt a sensation through his whole body as though insupportable weight was bearing down on him from above, and inward on all sides. He wanted desperately to stand up: to throw out his arms and feel no walls. To toss back his head and see the sky. He wanted to run with the wind in his face. He felt that if he did not get out he would die. And he knew that he could never get out.

Padgett was easing his way around a corve which almost blocked the working. Beyond it, the feeble lamplight fell upon the coal-face: the end of the tunnel.

A solid wall of coal, to be hacked out with pick, chisel and shovel. The tunnel would grow longer, inch by inch, day by day, so that the steel mills might continue to roar.

Padgett groped among the scattered tools and chunks of coal and pulled out a short, thick crutch, like the wooden part of a catapult. He stuck the leg of this into the floor, and lay down on his back, so that his neck rested in the 'v' of the crutch. His head was thus supported some inches from the floor. He had stripped off his shirt and now wore only breeches and cap. He held a short pick in his hands. 'Get the shovel and fill up that corve!' he said. Jimmy found the shovel. He pushed the worn blade into the coal that lay heaped around his master, and lifted it to the corve. His arms could barely raise the laden shovel, and it trembled, so that some of the coals fell off. 'Keep it steady, ye slack brat!' snarled Padgett. 'There'll be another load ready before ye get back, so get shovellin'.' And he turned his attention to the face, hacking away with short, strong movements of his bulging arms, and grunting with the effort.

Jimmy shovelled. He had to work kneeling; sitting back on his heels. And even so, he had to keep his head bent forward to avoid striking the roof. His knees, back and arms ached abominably. He gasped for breath and his lungs found only hot, foul air. It seemed hours until the corve was filled, and he dared to stop. And when the load was at last heaped to within a few inches of the roof, another corve-full lay around his master: hacked out with a sound like thunder in this oppressive space. He dropped the shovel and allowed his arms to hang limply, the black, blistered hands lying like dead things on the floor. He moved his aching neck from side to side. The blood pounded in his ears.

The hacking stopped.

'Move!' screamed Padgett, raising his head from the crutch. 'Get harnessed up and go!'

'Harnessed?' gasped Jimmy.

Padgett rolled over and came to his knees. 'Get round the front of the corve,' he yelled, and pushed the pick-handle into the boy's ribs. Jimmy winced, and scrambled quickly round the laden corve. Padgett followed with the lamp. 'Put this on!' He held a broad, thick leather belt with a brass buckle. Jimmy buckled it round his waist. There was an iron ring near the buckle with a thick, black chain fastened to it. The chain ended in a hook. Padgett passed the chain down between Jimmy's legs and fastened the hook to a ring in the corve. He lit a stump of candle and stuck it among the coals. 'You pull it like that till t'main road,' he snapped, angry at having had to pause in his work. 'Then unharness and push from behind on t'rails. Leave it at shaft-bottom, where ye came down this morning. There'll be empty corves there. Bring one back. And don't stop to talk to anyone! This pit is crawlin' with idle brats, but trammers of mine don't have time to talk!'

Jimmy, on hands and knees, strained forward. The chain bit into his groin, but the corve didn't move. 'Get yer knees off the floor!' yelled Padgett, from beyond the corve. Jimmy lifted himself on to his toes and hands and lunged forward again. The corve rolled forward a little, lurching on the uneven floor. Jimmy moved agonisingly, pushing at the floor with the balls of his feet. His breeches brushed the roof as he went slowly forward. The corve gained a little momentum, and Jimmy found that if he did not move his feet quickly enough, it ran into his heels, taking the skin off. He was trying to remember how far he had crawled up the working this morning. He thought it was about a hundred yards. The sweat poured down his forehead, carrying coaldust into his eyes, but he dared not stop to wipe it away. The belt was hurting his stomach. The corve rumbled, scrunching bits of coal under its iron wheels. A hundred yards! It seemed a hundred miles before Jimmy crawled out into the main road. He knelt there, beside the track, gasping and swept with nausea. It had seemed hot in the main road this morning, but compared to the heat in the working, it was cool.

He dared not linger long. As soon as the feeling of sickness passed, he scrambled to his feet, and after great effort got the laden corve on to the rails. Pushing from behind was comparatively easy and the corve rumbled along quickly. Jimmy came opposite to the closed road, where curiosity caused him to pause. It looked like any other of the workings. He fetched the candle and, after glancing in both directions, and listening, squatted and thrust a blackened arm into the forbidden mouth.

There was nothing to see. The dim light fell on a pine prop, bent and splitting a little way in. Somewhere far away water was dripping. What had Trapper Joe seen in there, which caused him to fear for his life? Jimmy's curiosity tugged at him, but nothing could induce him to go alone into that thick darkness.

It was hard, pushing in the side-gate. Wherever there were no rails it was hard. The gate rumbled open as he strained toward it.

'Joe?' whispered Jimmy, and the whisper echoed away along invisible walls.

'Aye.'

'I . . . I wondered if you were still there,' stuttered Jimmy.

A short yelp of mirth. 'Well, if I ain't, summat else opened t'gate for ye!' Jimmy took his candle again and held it to the hole in the wall. Joe was still grinning.

'What's in closed road?' hissed Jimmy. Joe's grin dissolved.

'Ye'd better move on, Jimmy,' he said. 'Mr Padgett don't like waitin'.'

Jimmy crouched, advancing into the hole. 'Tell me why you're afraid,' he said menacingly.

'I'm saying nowt.' Joe's voice was sullen, then urgent as he went on, 'Look, Jimmy; it's for yer own good. Forget about closed road. Mr Padgett'll be seekin' another trammer if ye don't. And he'll be seekin' one anyway, if ye don't move yerself with that corve!'

Jimmy grabbed the small boy's shoulder with his free hand. His frustration exploded, so that he shouted, 'You can't just sit here waiting for them to kill you; if you saw something, why don't you tell someone; someone outside?'

Joe wriggled free. 'For God's sake 'old yer noise!' he

hissed. A small hand darted from the shadow and the candle was plucked from Jimmy's hand.

Joe held it near to his face. 'Back out of this 'ole or I'll blow this light out,' he said softly. 'How'd ye like to find yer way back without it?'

Jimmy shook his head. 'No! All right, Joe; I'm going. Give me the candle.' He stuck it back among the coals. 'I think you're a fool, Trapper Joe,' he said to the darkness.

'A little 'un,' came the reply. 'And 'ere goes a bigger one with corve an' candle. 'Ave a care, new boy, or they'll put ye underground for ever!' When he returned with the empty corve, Joe opened his gate and said nothing.

The day passed with agonising slowness: a blur of coaldust, sweat and cramp, until Jimmy could no longer remember how many corves he had hauled. Once, he was permitted to rest for a few minutes, crouching in the working, to eat his oatcake smeared with lard, and damp with gritty sweat. Padgett swigged from a bottle, and passed it over with a grunt. Jimmy gulped the warm water thankfully, washing the harsh grit from his throat. Then a cob of coal hurled at his head told him to be on his way again, and the palpable darkness swallowed him like death.

At last it ended. He returned with a corve to find Padgett crouching among the coals, mopping his face with a black rag. 'All right; that's it,' he growled. 'Yer finished for today.' He looked sidelong at the exhausted boy. 'Ye'd best be quicker, though, to-morrow.'

They crawled down the working and into the main road, which was loud with weary men. Padgett stopped, talking in low tones with another collier. Jimmy leaned on the rough wall. Dim figures brushed past, muttering. The darkness had coloured patterns on it, swirling before his tired eyes. Every part of him hurt. His feet and knees were raw, and the palms of his hands. His nails were split and blackened. There was a weal across his stomach where the harness had been. His head ached from pushing the corves. He put up a hand, feeling for the bald patch, but his hair, matted with grime, was still there.

Presently the other collier left. The road was deserted now, and Padgett growled, 'Come on.' Jimmy followed his master's lamp. He moved stiffly along between the rails, entering the side-gate. The gate stood open. 'Trapper Joe will have gone up,' he told himself. He was almost out of the side-gate when a faint noise caused him to whirl. Without a candle he could not be sure, but it seemed that a small figure was flitting away along the gate, toward the road he had just left. Jimmy turned and began to edge his way back the way he had come. Padgett trudged on without turning.

Jimmy knew that he would not have long: his master would miss him at the shaft-bottom and come seeking him. But he had to know what Trapper Joe was doing.

When he reached the far end of the side-gate, Joe had moved into the road. Jimmy could not see him: it was almost totally dark; but he could hear the scuffing of feet, and breathing. He moved out into the road, following the sounds. 'Joe must have cat's eyes,' he thought, as he moved with hands groping before him, 'from being in that hole all day.'

A sound just ahead made him stop. A scraping sound, followed by the flare of sudden light. He pressed to the wall. Joe was crouching by closed road, his head and shoulders inside. As Jimmy watched, the rest of the child's body went in. He waited a few seconds as the candle-light flickered away into the hole. Then he moved up, to crouch and peer inside. Joe's body was a hunched silhouette behind the candle. The roof props seemed more bent than before. Water dripped somewhere, and Joe's progress made a scraping sound. There was no other sound and nothing more to see.

Jimmy stood, leaning against the wall. If he followed Joe in, there was no way he could keep the child from seeing him. If he waited here until he came out, perhaps there would be some clue to what he had been doing. Perhaps he would hear something if he knelt just in the entrance.

He was about to do this when he became aware of sounds coming from the side-gate, and glancing wildly in that direction he saw moving light spilled out into the road. Fear washed through him, and he almost fell with the trembling in his legs. He looked desperately for a place to hide. The approaching light showed the entrance to another working a few yards beyond closed road. He dropped on all fours, moving swiftly; backing into the hole. His head was barely withdrawn when a man came out of the side-gate with a lamp. Jimmy peered out. A stocky, pink-faced man with clean breeches and polished boots. Not a collier. The thought flickered through Jimmy's mind. Perhaps he would go by. The man stopped by closed road and looked back. He seemed to be waiting. Jimmy pulled back his head, scarcely breathing. Joe was trapped. And what of himself? The last colliers would be going up now. Padgett would miss him at any moment, but he could not move while this man remained here. In the quiet, he could hear the man's breathing, and the sound of the winding gear far away. Would he ever ride the clatch-iron up into the cool air?

He started, as a loud cry reverberated through the pit. 'Mr Rawdon!'

The clatter of footsteps coming along the side-gate. Jimmy peered stealthily. Padgett's voice; and the big collier himself, running crouched behind his swinging lamp. 'Mr Rawdon: don't go in, sir! There's two brats loose in 'ere somewhere!'

The other man gasped and peered wildly all around, holding up his lamp. 'Brats? What brats?' he croaked. Padgett stumbled up to him.

'A new hurrier of mine and that Trapper Joe,' he snarled. 'They're still 'ere somewhere: I watched everyone up t'shaft, and they never went up.'

Rawdon, plainly agitated, snapped: 'Why can't you take more care? You *know* you must always be the last man up: that's what I pay you for.'

'Aye, Mr Rawdon, sir; I know. It's crowded though, at shaft-bottom at knockin' off time, and I just missed 'em.'

Rawdon gave an impatient snort. 'This is the second time in three weeks, Padgett. That trapper skulked around for some time before you missed him: I'm convinced he saw something.'

Padgett shrugged. 'I asked you to let me get rid of 'im,' he muttered.

Rawdon turned on the collier, trembling so that his lamp shook in his clenched hand. 'Look, Padgett,' he grated. 'I can't afford too many accidents down here: not with Croft always poking and prying around. Your killing that hurrier gave me no end of trouble. Two notes from that confounded man; *and* I had to pay five guineas to the brat's mother to quieten her.'

Jimmy stiffened with fear. He knew now what kind of accident had befallen his predecessor. He searched his reeling mind for a way out. He edged forward to observe the two men. They stood now in whispered conversation, and Jimmy could not make out the words. They were directly in front of closed road, their legs like bars over the hole. Had Joe heard Padgett's shout? Jimmy decided that he must have heard it. If he came down the working now, he would crawl right into them. If he stayed where he was, he would be caught when either of the men decided to go into closed road. And even if both men moved away, there was no way out of the pit except by the clatch-iron, which by now could only be manned by some ally of Padgett. To remain where he was, though, meant inevitable discovery also, and Jimmy knew that he would flee, though there was nowhere to go.

He edged forward further, until his shoulders were clear of the hole. The two men were still whispering. Jimmy's hand crabbed over the gritty floor, and found a small coal. Easing himself on to one elbow he drew back his arm and sent the coal spinning down the road. It passed the two men before striking the floor, and at the sound of it they whirled, holding out their lamps.

'There's one of 'em!' cried Padgett, starting towards the sound. Rawdon followed, both men going as quickly as the low roof permitted.

By the light from their receding lamps Jimmy saw a small figure emerge at once from closed road, and Joe came up towards his hiding place, moving soundlessly and glancing over his thin shoulder at the two silhouettes behind. He started at Jimmy's hiss. 'Joe!' Jimmy scrambled from his hole.

The smaller boy pressed a finger to his lips: an urgent plea for silence. He looked back. The men still faced the other way, swinging their lamps: muttering. Joe pressed his mouth to the other boy's ear. 'One way out: furnace shaft. That way.' He gestured toward the men.

Jimmy's heart lurched, in hope and in fear. 'Past them?' The question was a breath only: soundless.

Joe read it, nodding. He turned, creeping back toward closed road, signalling that Jimmy follow close. At the mouth he stooped, scooping chips from the floor and drawing back his arm, poised. 'Ready?' Jimmy nodded, although he wasn't.

Padgett was turning. The chips hissed and rattled, far up closed road. A thin arm in Jimmy's back, slamming him into the wall, opposite the hole. Both men were coming now, at a crouching lope. Padgett first. Jimmy heard him say, 'They're *in* there!' and Joe say, 'Ready?' again. This time he was. Padgett came level, eyes on the hole. Lamplight washed over the cowering boys, and Rawdon saw. 'Padgett! Here!' he cried, and Joe said, 'Go!'

Ducking Rawdon's arm, Jimmy was away at an awkward run into solid blackness. Joe behind, prodding, hissing, 'Go, go, go!' And behind again, the scrunch of heavy boots, and cursing, and swinging yellow light. A curve in the road. Jimmy cried out, blundering into the wall, and Joe pushed again, sobbing, 'Go, go, go!' Ahead now, a faint orange glow. Fire. A great brazier. ashy at its top, glowing still, further down. And above it, in the roof, a hole, chimney-like. Jimmy stopped before the hot iron. Joe pushed. 'Up!' he gasped, gesturing to the chimney. Heavy boots, rounding the curve.

'How?' The question was screamed. 'It's hot—red hot!'

'Go!' screamed back Joe, dragging him on to the hot metal. Jimmy, teeth gritted, climbed the iron basket, hands and feet seared, showering ash on the floor. Standing atop the settling cinders, head and shoulders in the stifling hole, he clawed desperately for a hold with his fingers, feeling Joe below, climbing.

A hold: a crack only, and greasy with soot. He strained, sobbing, drawing up his body by the strength of his trembling arms: jamming his back into one wall and his blistered feet into the other. He moved, gasping, upward, pushing with the friction-hold of his feet so that his back rasped up the rough wall a little way, then jamming there, moving his feet up one at a time until his knees were bent for another bone-cracking push. His head reeled. No air: fumes from the brazier filled the narrow chimney. A crash, below, and sharp curses, Joe, head brushing Jimmy's feet, incredibly laughing. 'Go, Jimmy!' came his cry, exultant now. Hard pressed, he had paused long enough to kick over the brazier.

Inching upward, shredding jacket and blisters on invisible walls. Inching upward: bending and straightening, bending and straightening, endlessly, like a caterpillar on a twig. The fumes were gone. Cold air washed down and Jimmy's head cleared. He looked up through sweat-stung eyes and saw the stars. One push more, and his hands found the rim. He was lying in grass. Sobbing, hurting in every part of his body, and lying in grass. Joe was there, crying, harshly, with a sound in it like triumph. But somewhere near, winding gear, grinding relentlessly. Winding on its thick, oily chain.

Joe stilled his sobs, listening. Then, 'Up! Get up!' he cried, the voice cracked and thin. 'They're coming up!'

Jimmy tottered to his feet, screwing his eyes in the direction of the winding gear. He could see nothing of it through the dark. His chest hurt with breathing. 'Where, Joe?' he gasped. 'Where can we go?'

'Mr Croft's.' Joe pointed to where a pale streak of road wound uphill through black woods. 'Mr Croft will help us: I've got something for 'im.' And he ran, stooped and ragged on his thin legs.

Without understanding, Jimmy followed. They gained the road before sounds of pursuit came to them. Jimmy glanced over his shoulder. People, running through the long grass towards the road. Two lamps. Shouting. Padgett barking orders. Jimmy stumbled on.

The road was deeply rutted. Water and sticky clay lay in the ruts. He heard Joe ahead, splashing and sucking through the mud. His head spun. Lights swirled behind his eyes. The men were on the road now, stumbling cursing the ruts. Jimmy forced his legs to go on, pounding the torn feet into the mud. His joints burned and his breathing was like sawing in his head. He was in darkness now, the road swallowed by the trees. The wood crowded in on both sides. The boots were closer now. He knew he could run no more. A bend in the road, just ahead, and through the trees a light. Joe, flicking in silhouette across the light. He no longer felt his feet. He could feel nothing now. There was light before him, coming closer, and light behind him, coming closer. And a thin voice in his head, saying go, go, go; rhythmically, relentlessly. On, between tall stone pillars where iron gates stood open. The road was a driveway now. Shush of running feet on deep chippings. A pale, wide stairway. Marble, cool and smooth. Up, up, up. Long stairway of cool, smooth marble. And then the marble stopped, and there was Joe, tiny against an immense door, pounding with small black fists.

Jimmy, on his knees in the porch, looked back. Lamps, down by the big iron gates. Murmurings, and a shout. Argument, under the dark trees. A lantern advancing a little in the driveway, then going back.

Joe stopped pounding. A light was moving behind the glass. Coming along the passage. A dim figure behind the door, bending. Bolts scraping back. The door opened, a crack only, and a lamp was in the crack, with a woman's face above it. 'What is it?' The voice was sharp, impatient. She scowled at the small black faces, the ragged clothes. 'What do you want?'

'Please, Missus,' gasped Joe. 'We got a message for Mr Croft.'

The woman made a sound, half querying, half impatient. 'Message? For Mr Croft? You?'

Joe glanced fearfully over his shoulder. The lamps were coming slowly up the drive. 'Please, Missus: it's very important. Them men are after us.'

The woman made no move to open the door further. She raised the lamp, peering down the drive. 'Them's colliers,' she snapped. 'And you're runaway pit-brats, I shouldn't wonder. Coming 'ere with yer stories! Well, Mr Croft's away in London, and ye needn't think I'm going to help ye: I'm not so soft as the master. Now be off with ye, before them colliers come tramplin' all over master's lawns.'

The door slammed and a bolt went home as Joe, desperate, threw his puny body against it. 'Missus! Please, Missus, wait: I've got summat to show ye!' The lamp receded, bobbing away along the passage.

The colliers, grouped half-fearful in the drive, saw the door close, and the boys still on the porch. A word from Padgett and they surged forward.

Jimmy saw and cried, 'Joe! They're coming!'

Joe spun round, his eyes darting this way and that over the dark gardens. Then, 'This way,' he hissed, pulling Jimmy down the stairway. They swerved to the left, running across a smooth lawn. Behind, the colliers were shouting. Across the lawn and into the rhododendrons beyond. Crashing through wet foliage, panting.

'Where?' Jimmy gasped. Joe made no reply, jinking through the shrubs. Jimmy followed the small figure, dim among the shadows.

The rhododendrons ended and they were on a long downslope of lawn. Water glinted ahead. Joe swerved right, where a path followed the lake's edge. Ahead Jimmy saw a clump of trees grouped around a wooden shelter. He looked back. There was nobody yet on the downslope, although light moved among the black shrubs and voices, querulous, angry, punctured the soft darkness. They reached the trees. The shelter was an open-fronted summer-house facing the lake. Joe walked all round it, looking upward. Then 'Come on!' he hissed, and began to shin up on to the roof. The rustic poles were easily climbed, and the boys lay along the mossy roof, watching the rhododendrons.

A collier was on the slope, holding up his lamp and shouting something back into the shrubs. Another lamp appeared. The first man pointed to the path that rimmed the lake in both directions. Others joined them, and the boys could make out Padgett's voice, snapping out orders. The cluster of lamps split into two. One party went towards the farther end of the lake. The other came towards the trees. Jimmy pressed his cheek into the moss and stopped his breath. The colliers saw the shelter and two of them came on at a run, holding up their lamps to the doorway. There was a chink in the roof by Jimmy's face and Padgett was four feet below him, peering under the bench which was all the shelter contained. The other man swung his lamp towards the rafters, screwing his eyes into the cobwebbed gloom. Jimmy stiffened. His heart seemed to be pounding the roof. After a moment the lamp was lowered and the two men joined the others at the lake. Mutterings, and then they moved off, following the path.

The boys lay silent until the lamps were dim with distance and the voices faint. They lowered themselves to the ground.

'I know an old pit,' breathed Joe. 'We can 'ide there till they stop lookin'.'

Jimmy gazed in the direction of the lamps. 'What is it, in closed road? What have you got for Mr Croft?' Joe pushed a black hand into his ragged pocket and held it out. Something glistened in the palm. Jimmy took it.

'A button? What's the use of this? What does it mean?'

Joe took back the button, and said: 'There's a man in closed road, all chained up. I seen 'im before, but I was so scared I didn't go near. 'E's a gentleman; I know by 'is clothes. 'E pulled this off 'is coat an' gave it to me.'

'Why did you bring it for Mr Croft? Why him?'

'Mr Croft 'elps pit brats. I've 'eard colliers talkin' about 'im. I've 'eard Mr Fawcett say, " 'E'll end all this, wi' God's 'elp, will Mr Croft." An' 'e meant brats workin' in t'pit an' all.' He glanced around. 'No time to talk: come on.' And he flitted away, back towards the rhododendrons.

At the edge of the lawn they stopped. A woman was in an upstairs window, looking out. The lamp behind her cast a shadow enormous across the grass. After a moment she moved away, and they ran, stooped, across the front of the house and down toward the gates. At the gates they paused, listening. Faint shouts came from various parts of the grounds. None of the colliers seemed to be near by. The two runaways went out on to the rutted road and walked down a way, in silence, until Joe led his companion into the trees beside the track.

Soon they were crossing open fields, and at length Joe stopped beside a yawning hole in the ground. It was spanned by a rusted winding gear, but there was only a short length of chain, and no clatch-iron. 'There's a ladder in the shaft,' Joe said. 'Fastened in the side. It's safe: I've been down before.' And he went on his knees in the long grass, feeling along the rim. ' 'Ere it is. Just feel it with yer 'ands, then turn round an' get yer foot on it like this.' Joe slithered over the edge, feet first. When only the pale blob of his face was visible Jimmy knelt down. 'Turn round.' Joe's voice echoed a little as he moved down into the shaft. 'Put yer foot over, an' I'll guide it to the ladder.' Jimmy turned and, gripping the coarse turf with his hands, lowered his legs into space. He felt a hand on his ankle and then a rung under his toes. He lowered himself, trembling, feet groping from rung to rung.

The shaft smelled dank. The sides were slimy and crumbling in places. The ladder was coated thickly with rust which came off in Jimmy's hands and drifted down into the blackness. The descent seemed endless, but after a long time, Joe said hollowly, 'I'm down. It's water, but not deep!'

Jimmy's foot went down, seeking the next rung, and the cold shock made him wince. Standing ankle-deep at shaft bottom, he could not see Joe. He was splashing somewhere near. 'Joe?'

'Over 'ere.' Jimmy waded toward the sound. 'It goes up 'ere: it's dry.' He put out his arms, until his hands touched Joe's jacket. The floor sloped upwards and he was on mud. Joe plucked at his sleeve, pulling him further into the invisible road. 'Duck yer 'ead,' he said. 'It's dry further up.' They stumbled on until the floor became dusty. It was warm. The air felt thick. 'Sit down 'ere.' Jimmy sank down thankfully. His head was muzzy with tiredness. It seemed days since he had slept. He saw a picture in his head of the boys' dormitory where he had slept every night since he could remember. The rows of narrow beds down each wall, so close they almost touched one another. The rough grey blankets and prickly straw mattresses. The lime-washed walls and high, narrow windows. The Union Workhouse; a place dreaded, he had heard, by those who lived beyond its walls. Yet now he found himself longing for that hard iron bed with its thin blanket. At least there you knew what was going to happen tomorrow. There would be food; not enough, but some. And work; too much, and deadly monotonous. But no danger: no probability of violent death. These things he felt dimly, as he lay in the unseen dust, head resting on his arms. Joe was breathing softly near by.

'Joe?' He heard the small boy grunt: perhaps he had been asleep. 'What are we to do, Joe, with Mr Croft in London?' Joe grunted again.

'Go to London and find 'im.'

Jimmy gasped. 'We could never do that, Joe: London's a very big place, so I've heard, and far away.'

'There's nowt else we can do.'

'We could show the button to somebody here.'

Joe laughed shortly. ' 'Ere? They'd not believe us: we're just runaway brats.'

'There's the button.'

'You can find a button in t'road!'

'We could wait here till Mr Croft comes home.'

'We'd starve to death: anyway the Gentleman'll die in closed road if we wait.'

Jimmy was silent. Who was the man in closed road? Why was he there? The questions swirled round inside his head. London! They would never get to London with everybody hunting them as runaways. And even if they did get there, how would they find Mr Croft? And if they did find him, why should he believe them? 'You can find a button in the road,' Joe had said.

Joe was sleeping. Jimmy lay for a while, listening to his even breathing. Then the lids fell over his own eyes, and he slipped away.

6

WHEN JOE AWOKE, he crawled round the still sleeping Jimmy and went down to shaft-bottom. The sky was a bright disc far above so he knew that it was day. They would be searching in earnest now. He was hungry. He turned and waded back to dry ground. He wished there was a candle: the blackness was total. Jimmy awoke as Joe came up. 'It's day,' said Joe. 'They'll be lookin' all over now.'

'I hope they won't come down here.' Jimmy's voice from the dark.

Joe laughed, without humour. 'They'd not come *down*, Master Jimmy: they'd fetch men to fill in t'shaft if they thought we were 'ere.'

Jimmy shuddered. 'I'd sooner go up and take my chance.'

'No!' Joe hissed. 'We'd not 'ave a chance. I've seen brats run away before: they always catch 'em in daylight. We'll wait till night: they'll think we're clear away by then.'

'Well; I just hope they don't think of this place, that's all,' whispered Jimmy. They sat hugging their knees, listening. Water dripped, far off. The day passed slowly.

When Joe came back and reported gathering night above, Jimmy got up stiffly and they went hunching down the road and into the water. As he went, Jimmy breathed a prayer of thankfulness that their hiding-place had not been discovered. If they got out of this, he told himself, he would never go underground again.

Joe went up first. At the rim, he raised his head cautiously and looked all around. The sky was still pink in the west but the land lay under deepening shadow. Croft Hall was a silhouette on the hill.

Nobody was visible on the road. Far off, some people were hoeing. Rawdon Pit was invisible behind trees.

He hauled himself out, and lay in the grass. Jimmy came up. Joe pressed a finger to his lips for silence. They lay in the grass and watched the darkness spreading.

When they could no longer see the trees on the hillside they stood and crept catlike through the grass towards the road. They stayed in the fringe of trees, following the road but not venturing out upon it.

'Which way is London?' asked Jimmy.

'This road goes by Dewsbury,' Joe replied. 'That's on t'way to London.' They moved on in silence. Once a cart approached, and they lay down until it had gone by. The carter was singing to himself.

By the time they arrived at the point where the trees ended it was quite dark. The road wound now through the town, and Joe led the way on a long detour across fields, keeping the town lights far away on their right hand. Slowly the lights fell away behind, and Joe swung right until they found the road again. They went carefully upon the road, listening all the time. Now and then small groups of people came up, making for the town, and the runaways lay in the ditch until they had passed. After a while, there were no more people. The stars appeared and a cold half-moon. Jimmy wrapped his arms around his stomach. 'I'm hungry,' he said.

Joe grinned. 'There's food all around, Master Jimmy.'

'Where?' Jimmy's voice was eager.

'In t'fields. Once, I went to Dewsbury, to t'fair, and there was mangels and cabbages and crab-apples both sides of the road.'

The road here ran between hawthorn hedges and they searched until they found a gap. The field was planted with swedes. Joe grabbed a handful of leaves and pulled one up. Wet clay clung to the bulbous root. He sat down under the hedge and fetched out his knife. He scraped away the soil and cut off the leaves. Then he cut the swede into thick yellow slices and peeled off the purple rind. They ate ravenously, looking all the while, and listening. The night was silent. When they had eaten, and Joe had pushed the discarded pieces into the hedge bottom, they crawled back on to the road and walked on.

Presently, from the top of a hill they saw the lights of a town. 'Dewsbury,' said Joe. 'It must be.' They came to a stone beside the road, with a name on it, but neither boy could read. 'We'll go round the town, like before,' said Joe.

Jimmy groaned. 'I *can't* get over any more fences or through any more hedges tonight, Joe. It's late: it will be safe to go through the streets.'

Joe shrugged. 'Through t'streets then,' he said. 'But if I say run: run!' They entered the town. Most of the houses were in darkness. The boys hugged the buildings, flitting from pool to pool of deep shadow. A hiss from Joe! A man! Coming along the street. The runaways darted into a doorway, pressing back. The man carried a cane; he was drunk. He tottered by, muttering to himself. The boys slipped from the doorway and went on. They rounded a bend and ahead was a building with brightly lighted windows. There were people standing around, talking loudly, and music came from somewhere inside. Joe pulled Jimmy into an alley. 'We'll 'ave to go round behind that,' he hissed. 'It's a tavern.' They padded along the alley. They were about to emerge on to the road at the farther end, when there came the sound of voices. They froze. Jimmy peered round the corner. By the back wall of the tavern stood a group of men. They were looking at a poster. As the boys listened, one of the men began to read, hesitantly:

> Ten guineas reward, is offered by the undersigned, in return for information regarding the whereabouts of two runaway pit boys, wanted at Bradford for theft.

The man went on to read out descriptions of the wanted boys, which left no doubt in Jimmy's mind as to whom the poster described. The man's recital ended with 'Signed: H. H. Rawdon, Proprietor, Rawdon Colliery.'

The runaways stared at each other aghast. 'Theft?' stammered Joe. 'We didn't steal nowt.'

Jimmy shook his head. 'No, but who's to know that? Everyone will be on the lookout. Ten guineas! Anyone would turn us in for ten guineas.'

The men were dispersing; going off in twos and threes, discussing the poster. The words 'ten guineas' could be heard in most of the groups as they passed the alley where the boys stood pressed into the shadows. Nobody turned into the alley, and when the men had passed on, the boys stepped out on to the street and crept past the rear of the tavern, gazing at the fresh poster as they passed it.

By the time they came again into open country the runaways had seen a number of the bills posted on walls and posts. They became even more cautious, dropping into the ditch at the slightest sound, and making wide detours around every cottage light.

Around midnight, cloudbanks drifted in to hide the moon and a light drizzle set in. Jimmy turned up the collar of his jacket, shivering. 'Let's find a barn or summat, and go to sleep,' he said dully.

Joe shook his head. 'No. We can only move at night. We've got to get as far away as we can before daylight. We'll sleep in t'daytime.' They trudged on.

Dawn broke on a grey world. Cloud hung unbroken across the sky, and misty drizzle hid the fields, slanting endlessly down the wind. Joe wiped dank hair from dull eyes and gazed over the hedge. A stone's throw away, the trees were ghostly blurs, and beyond that everything merged into a milky obscurity. He glanced at Jimmy shuffling half-sleeping through the yellow mud. 'Nobody's goin' to see us on such a morning,' he said. 'We could go on a bit.'

Jimmy groaned. 'My feet's sore. I want to go to sleep.'

'The further we get, the better. London's a long way.'

'Aye: I know it. A long way.' They went on in silence. Presently the rain stopped and a cockcrow far off, reminded Joe that people would soon be about their daily business. He looked around. Away to his left a low hill swelled out of the fields, with trees at its crown. He plucked Jimmy's sodden sleeve. 'We can 'ide up there,' he said, pointing. 'We'd better get over t'fields before t'farmer's about.' They found a hole in the hedge and made their way across wet ploughland towards the hill. Somewhere a dog was barking. They kept to the hedgerows, walking crouched. Their clothing clung wetly to their backs and their teeth chattered incessantly. The ploughland ended and they were climbing through long grass. Halfway up, Jimmy paused and looked back. A farmhouse was visible now, tucked into a fold in the land, but nobody was in the yard. They reached the trees. The ground beneath them was relatively dry; a carpet of dank-smelling leaf-mould. Here and there, bracken grew between out-crops of grey rock. They found a dry place in an over-hang and squeezed into it.

'Should we keep a lookout?' asked Joe wearily.

Jimmy yawned. 'I don't suppose anyone comes up here,' he said. 'But anyway, I'm too cold to sleep.'

For a long time he lay in the bracken, watching the breeze stirring the birch boughs. Sounds reached him from time to time from a great way off: the bark of a dog; a clanking of pails; the rumble of a coach on the road. Joe slept, despite the cold, and presently, warmed a little by the closeness of his companion's body, Jimmy slept too.

The pump-handle clanked and water gushed into the pail. When it was full, the farmer straightened up, grunting. Two men were standing at the yard gate.

'Can ye spare us a minute, Mister?' one of them called.

The farmer made no reply, but went slowly over to the gate, his boots squishing in the deep mud. They were townmen. Thin, with pale faces and hungry eyes. One of them held a rolled paper in his hand.

'How can I help ye?' grunted the farmer. He was a busy man. The man with the paper unrolled it and held it out for him to see.

'We're after these two thieves,' he said. The farmer glanced at the paper.

'I can't read that,' he growled. 'What two thieves?'

'Two pit-brats,' put in the other man. 'They stole from their master and run away.'

The farmer shrugged. 'What's that to me?' he growled. 'I've cares enough of my own.'

'There's ten guineas reward,' said the first man. 'And the brats is on your land.'

'I've seen nobody,' grunted the farmer. 'And I've been about since dawn.'

The man pointed to the hill. 'Over there. They went up just at first light. We've followed 'em from Dewsbury.'

The farmer stroked his chin. 'Ten guineas you said: you'd have to cross my fields.' He gave the townmen a meaningful look.

'We'll give two guineas if we take 'em on your land.'

'Done!' said the farmer. 'Wait, and I'll fetch my gun.' He strode off into the house, reappearing with a shotgun under his arm. 'Follow me: I'll take you the shortest way.' The three set out towards the hill. The farmer strode ahead, and the townmen, footsore and wet, trudged behind.

At the foot of the hill the farmer stopped, waiting until the townmen came up with him. 'One of you better go round the hill,' he growled. 'And wait t'other side, lest they hear us coming and run.' The two muttered together a moment, then the one with the poster set off at a trot around the base of the hill. When he was out of sight the farmer led the way up.

Jimmy stirred and jerked awake. A bird was screaming loudly in the trees. He sat up, stiffly, listening. Joe moved, groaning. 'What's up?'

'Sh!' hissed Jimmy. He crawled from beneath the rock and stood up, head cocked on one side. A rhythmic swishing, as of somebody walking in long grass. A grunt, and a mumbled word. Jimmy whirled. 'Joe! Someone's coming; run!'

Joe rolled out from the overhang and scrambled erect, eyes wild. 'This way!' cried Jimmy, and began to run. They crashed through the bracken, jinking between trees. Behind, somebody roared, 'Stop! Stop or I fire!' They ran on.

A crash, and hiss of pellets in the foliage. They were out of the trees, going downward; plunging, arms out, stumbling. Jimmy tripped, rolled, and came to his feet again, leaping down. Joe, arms flailing, eyes and mouth wide; half running, half falling. Down, down. As they reached the foot a man rose from the grass swinging a cudgel. Joe was almost on him, rushing down, unable to check his plunge. The man raised his club. Jimmy yelled a warning and Joe swerved. The cudgel clipped his shoulder. He staggered, recovered, and went off over level ground. The man came at Jimmy, who swerved in mid-flight and made across the slope, gasping, head back, mouth agape. The man bounded to cut him off: to keep him on the slope. Jimmy glanced upward. Two men, coming down, slithering. A gun. A glance downward. Joe, plunging over ploughland, well clear. Jimmy stopped, sobbing. He was cut off. The clubman was coming up. Above him the other two had split; one to come down behind, the other before him. One chance: a last, futile ploy. He stood, shoulders heaving, until they came level with him, closing in, believing him spent; then he whirled and scrambled upward; upward toward the summit again, lungs bursting, legs on fire. They were below him now, shouting, scrambling up. The farmer stopped, levelling his fowling-piece. Jimmy heard the sharp, metallic click. 'Stop! Or I'll pick ye off like a hen on a fence!' The slope was bare and the man could not miss. Wearily, Jimmy stopped and turned, raising his arms. The townmen looked hungry as he came down towards them. Joe, tiny with distance, paused, looking back; then turned and ran into a wood.

7

HIS SHOULDERS HURT and his lungs burned, but he ran on until he was deep among the trees. There, under an old oak, he threw himself down, gasping painfully. His legs felt like water. His head spun and nausea washed through him. They had taken Jimmy. He screwed up his eyes, seeing again the small figure on the hillside, and the others, closing in . . .

He was alone. Alone, with a price on his head, and an impossible journey ahead of him. How could he finish alone what had to be done? Who would watch while he slept? Perhaps now he could only take his story, and his button, to the law officers, and hope that they might believe him. But they wouldn't. He knew they wouldn't. Mr Rawdon would say that he had stolen something and was making up a story to save himself. He would go to prison. He might be transported. Or worse: Mr Rawdon might have him killed. Mr Fawcett then? Tom Fawcett was a kindly man, as colliers go. But no: he might listen, but he was scared of Charlie Padgett, like everybody else. He wouldn't do anything.

Joe rolled over in the grass, taking out the button. He was so ill, the man in closed road. Coughing behind his gag, and his eyes sunken and feverish. He might be dead by now. Would be dead by the time Joe got to London. But he had no other chance: only Joe could save him. And there was Jimmy. Jimmy, in Mr Rawdon's hands. Joe sat up, pushing the button back into his pocket. He had to get to Mr Croft. 'I don't even know what 'e looks like,' he said aloud. His voice sounded very small, here in the wood.

The sickness had passed. Joe got to his feet. In his flight he had become quite lost. He had to find the road again; he must know where he was so that he could continue his journey when it grew dark. He found the edge of the wood, and moved round it, keeping just within the trees and looking out over the fields. Presently he saw the road and the wooded hill from which he had fled. Nothing stirred there now. He could see the farm, too. The yard was empty, except for black specks of chickens pecking around the pump. Joe groaned softly, clutching his stomach. His hunger was a cold lump inside him. When it became dark he would have to find food, or he would never reach London. He looked at the sky. The clouds were breaking up, and there was plenty of daylight left. He found a dry place beneath the roots of a fallen tree and curled up there to await the night.

'Ow!' Jimmy yelled. His arm was twisted up his back, held there by one of his captors.

'Move!' snarled the man. 'We 'aven't got all day.' They stumbled over the sticky furrows, making for the farm. The other man was haggling with the farmer.

'We'll need the loan of a trap. And a pony. Say another 'alf-guinea.'

'How do I know I'll ever see ye again; or my money?'

'Ye've got my word.'

The farmer laughed shortly. 'I'll send my lad with ye.'

'Pity we didn't take t'other 'un,' growled the town-man. 'Money'll be less, for one.'

At the farm Jimmy's hands were tied behind him. A hefty lad appeared in response to the farmer's shout, and was sent to fetch the trap. The farmer went into the yard and Jimmy was left with his captors in the stone-flagged kitchen.

'Sit down,' one of them said, nodding toward a bench. 'And don't think ye can give us the slip.' They stood with their backs to the fire, looking highly pleased with their morning's work. They were both thin, and their clothes were worn and frayed.

Jimmy sat down. 'We're not thieves,' he said defiantly. 'We've done no harm.' The man with the poster shrugged.

'That's nowt to us. Ten guineas, it says 'ere, and me and 'im without work these two years.' His companion nodded agreement.

'If you let me go, there's a man in London will pay more than ten guineas.'

Both men laughed. 'Oh aye: an' there's an old lady at Bath who'll leave me a thousand guineas in 'er will!' And the speaker slapped his thigh with the rolled paper in exaggerated mirth. Jimmy flushed.

'We were going to London to find Mr Croft,' he said. 'They've got a prisoner down Rawdon Pit. Help me, and Mr Croft will pay you.'

The man assumed an expression of mock horror. His eyes rolled. ' 'Ear that, Eli?' His voice trembled. 'A prisoner they've got, down Rawdon Pit!'

The man called Eli nodded, grinning. 'Terrible goin's on, Sam,' he said. 'Terrible!' Jimmy gritted his teeth, biting back his fury, and dropped his eyes.

'What, no more stories?' mocked Sam. 'No more tales of mystery and 'orror?'

'What's the good?' said Jimmy. 'You won't believe me: nobody will.'

'Oh, we believe ye, all right,' sneered Sam. 'Me an' Eli, we believe *everything* that runaway pit-brats tells us. But we sends 'em back just the same, 'cause we likes the feel of guineas in our 'ands. Very soothin', guineas is: very comfortin', like.'

Jimmy remained silent, knowing that further pleading would be futile. The lad brought the trap up to the gate and Jimmy was shoved across the muddy yard and made to lie curled on the boards. His ankles were bound. 'Lie still, and not a sound, if ye know what's good for ye,' ordered Sam. His humour had deserted him. The trap began to move, lurching and bouncing on the rough track. Jimmy winced. His elbows jarred on the boards and he was thrown from side to side between the muddy boots of his captors. Nobody spoke. Presently the pony slowed, and the trap swung out of the farm track and lurched northward up the rutted road.

Joe awoke from a fitful doze to find twilight seeping through the wood. The sun was a muddy ball on the horizon. A flock of starlings swept in from the fields, wheeling like a cloud above the wood and settling shrilly among the boughs. The ragged child lay for a while, listening to their clatter. 'I wish I was one of them,' he thought. 'They go everywhere together: 'undreds of 'em, and all the sky to fly in.' He saw in his mind the dismal hole in which he had crouched alone, day after day in the hot blackness. He gazed up through the leaves at the squabbling horde. 'I'd never be by miself, any more,' he mused.

Twilight deepened into darkness. He could no longer make out the shapes of the birds against the sky. They had stopped quarrelling and were still. He got to his feet. His head swam and he felt weak. He had eaten nothing since yesterday. He gazed through the gloom at the distant farm. There was a dog there. He had heard it. But he had to have food. Not just a raw swede: real food. He thought of the oatcakes he ate in the early mornings, before he set off for the pit. Hot oatcakes, and Mrs Law in the candlelight, knifing a layer of lard on to them for him. Mrs Law kept the house he lived in with eleven other pit boys. They slept on straw on the floor, covering themselves with old clothes. They said that Mrs Law was rich, because Mr Rawdon gave her money for beds and blankets, and she didn't buy them. But she made good oatcakes, and thick porridge. And Mr Rawdon probably didn't give her money, anyway. He knuckled his eyes, rubbing away the thoughts, and crept stealthily out of the trees. The moon was not up yet and it was quite dark. He kept near the hedges as he approached the farm. When he reached the yard gate the dog was still silent. He peered into the yard. A window spilled light on to the strawy mud, and a man was moving about behind the window. Joe could see him clearly, but he knew the man would not be able to see out very well. He would have to risk the dog: perhaps it was away rabbiting. He pushed the gate. It creaked a little, and he froze, but the man went on moving about inside. Joe slipped into the yard and ghosted across to the house wall, flattening himself there. The lighted window was right beside him. He peered, cautiously. A long table of black, shiny wood, and chairs around. The man was coming out of another room carrying a plate with meat on it. There was bread on the table and a pitcher of milk. His hunger burned. He peered again. The man was going away into the other room. After a moment he came back with some cheese, which he set on the table. Then he took a watch from his pocket, looked at it, and came toward the window. Joe ducked back, his heart pounding. He watched the patch of light on the ground. The man's shadow was printed on it. He was standing still, peering out into the night. Joe pressed himself to the wall, scarcely breathing. The shadow moved away and Joe looked in. The man had his watch out again and was frowning. He seemed to be waiting for somebody. As Joe watched, he went out of the room and reappeared with a hat on his head, and carrying a lantern. He lit the lantern and moved toward the outside door. Joe crabbed rapidly back along the housefront until he reached the corner. The door was opening. He darted round the corner and flattened again, holding his breath. The door slammed and the lantern bobbed across the yard. The farmer pulled open the gate and went through. He stood there a moment looking towards the road, and then he went off slowly down the track. Joe breathed his relief and slid round to the housefront again. The lamp still burned inside the room. There seemed to be nobody else about. He darted swiftly to the door and lifted the latch. His hunger made him reckless—a push, the door swung back, and he was inside.

He crossed rapidly to the table, ducking so as not to show himself in the window, and grabbed the hunk of meat. He laid it on the stone floor and slashed chunks out of it with his knife. Cramming one chunk into his mouth and the others into his pockets, he left the ragged bone and reached for the bread. This he tore up and stuffed into his pockets also. He raised his head to the window, but could see only reflections. Standing, he scooped up the cheese and tucked it under his arm. With this and the milk-pitcher he half-ran for the door, heart pounding, and peered out. Nobody. Sobbing with tension and with thankfulness, he went clumsily across the yard, sloshing milk into the mud at every step. At the gate he shot a glance towards the road. The farmer was standing at the end of the track, faintly visible in the glow from his lantern. Joe crossed the track and squeezed through the hedge, losing more milk. He hobbled gleefully over the ploughland with his booty, crossing two fields before he sank down at last in the shelter of a hawthorn to eat.

He ate quickly, taking copious draughts from the pitcher between mouthfuls. The vessel was almost empty when he heard the rattle of a vehicle down on the road and, standing, saw the lantern-hung trap turning into the track. He drained the pitcher and tossed it into the hedge, wiping the back of his hand across his mouth. His pockets still bulged with food. For the first time since his journey had begun he felt that he might really be able to complete it: felt, in fact, something which, indefinable, he had never felt in his life before. Here was the road before him, leading towards he knew not what. Behind him an avaricious man rode unwittingly toward his ruined supper. All around, the darkness covered the land, and nobody saw half so well in the dark as Trapper Joe. He went along the hedgerow, whistling softly, and turned south along the empty road.

8

THE SKYLIGHT was small and streaked with soot, so that the corners of the attic were dim. Jimmy shifted his position a little on the dusty boards. His wrists were still tied and he supported himself on elbows bruised by his journey. Hugh Rawdon regarded him coldly from the chest upon which he was sitting.

'The men who brought you here said you told them you were making for London, to find Mr Croft.' Rawdon paused. Jimmy gazed into his florid face and said nothing. The big man leaned forward, hands on knees. 'Have you any idea how big London is?' he sneered. 'You might search for months and never find the person you seek. You are a fool, Booth. And do not imagine that your little companion will get very far: since I know where he is going, it will be a simple matter to have him waylaid.' Jimmy remained silent, cursing himself inwardly for having told his captors about London. Now they would get Joe, too.

Rawdon stood and began pacing the floor, hands clasped behind him. 'What did he tell you, the man in closed road?'

'Nothing,' said Jimmy. 'I never saw him.' Rawdon stopped his pacing, bending over him.

'Your friend then: this trapper. What did the man tell *him*?' Jimmy shook his head.

'I don't know. We were running: Joe didn't tell me.' Rawdon's boot crashed on the boards. His face was twisted with fury.

'The money! A message for Croft about the money!' Jimmy's blank expression was genuine.

'Money? I know nothing of that, sir. We didn't steal anything.'

Rawdon lifted a foot and kicked him, hard. 'Come, you lying little blackguard; the message!' Jimmy doubled up, gasping. Rawdon stood over him, hands on hips. 'Come now: no shamming. 'Twas a gentle kick.' He bent closer and roared: 'The message!'

'I don't know,' gasped Jimmy, through his teeth.

'Very well: I have no more time to waste with you. Your master shall ask you now.' He strode to the door, flinging it open. 'Padgett! Here's a 'prentice of yours won't answer me.' Jimmy heard boots on the stairs. Padgett was in the doorway. The two men muttered together, then Rawdon went down. Padgett slammed the door and walked towards Jimmy. He was limping. 'D'ye see this foot?' he grated. 'It's broke. Summat fell on it down Rawdon Pit: no; it didn't fall: it got *pushed*. Summat with 'ot coals in it.' He bent swiftly, seizing Jimmy by the collar, lifting him. 'Ye'll tell *me* what I want to know, or I'll throttle the life out of ye!' Jimmy writhed in his grasp, helpless.

'I . . . I can't,' he gasped. 'I don't know about any money.'

Padgett let go, and the boy fell limply, crying out as his forehead struck the floor. The collier looked down at him, unbuckling the thick belt around his waist. 'Ye'll talk, if ye know what's good for ye,' he hissed. Through a blur of tears, Jimmy watched him wrap the buckle-end around his great fist.

He was lying on the floor and his mouth was full of dust. He opened his eyes. Darkness. He moved and gasped with the pain. His whole body throbbed with it. Except his hands. They were still tied, and he could not feel them. He gave up trying to move and lay, one cheek in the dust, listening to the hiss of rain on the skylight. It was cold and his hunger was a dull ache.

He thought about Joe. Where was Joe now? A feeling of hopelessness washed over him. Joe would be caught. He would never bring help. And tomorrow, when he still couldn't answer their questions, they would kill him. Nobody would ever know. They would say he ran off and was never seen again. Or there was another accident at the pit. The thoughts turned in his head, around and around.

Presently he heard footfalls and lay still, closing his eyes. Someone was talking on the stairs. Perhaps they were coming now to kill him. He bit his lip, trembling. The creaking came near. A key grated and the door opened. Lamplight.

'You, boy!' Rawdon. Jimmy lay still. 'Boy!' He heard the lamp being set down. Rawdon's voice again, a harsh whisper. 'See if he's . . . if Padgett's done for him, he'll pay; by God he shall!'

Somebody was bending over him. A hand on his cheek. 'He's alive, sir. Shall I bring water to revive him, sir?'

'Yes. And hurry.' The man who had touched him went off down the stairs. The chest creaked as Rawdon sat on it.

It seemed they did not intend to kill him. Not yet, anyway. The other man came back, bending over him again. He felt a wet cloth on his lips. He moaned and moved his head, as though just awakening. The man lifted his head and held a pot to his lips. Jimmy sucked in the cool water gratefully. He opened his eyes. 'That's enough, Wilkins. You can go now. Send Padgett up.'

Rawdon came and looked down at Jimmy, holding the lamp. The man called Wilkins went away, taking the pot with him. Jimmy screwed up his eyes in the lamplight. His head ached and he felt sick. Was Padgett coming to beat him again?

'Well,' said Rawdon sullenly. 'If you don't know about the money, Croft does, and if he won't speak to save himself, perhaps he will speak to save *you*: he shares his brother's concern for workhouse brats and the like!' He turned away as Padgett clumped up the stairs. 'Take the brat to the pit. Put him with Croft, and tell him the brat will be fed when he talks, and not before. And don't let anybody see you!'

Padgett grabbed Jimmy by the arm, hauling him to his feet. His head swam. If Padgett had not been holding him, he would have fallen down again. His back was one great bruise and his legs were stiff with cold. 'Move!' snarled Padgett, pushing the boy toward the door. He went down the stairs slowly, fighting nausea. Padgett was behind him. Rawdon brought the lamp, locking the attic door. There were three flights of stairs and then a long, dim corridor. Rawdon left them at the head of the corridor, and Padgett pushed Jimmy along it until they came to the kitchen. They left the house by the kitchen door, crossing the vegetable garden and leaving the grounds through a narrow door in the wall.

A steady rain fell and heavy cloud covered the sky. They trudged in silence. Padgett held Jimmy's arm in an iron grip. They met nobody on the muddy road. They passed a number of cottages, all in darkness. Presently Padgett jerked him to a halt at a cottage door.

'Not a word, d'ye hear?' he hissed, and knocked loudly on the door. They stood for a moment, listening to the hiss of the rain. Nothing stirred. Padgett growled and knocked again. Faint sounds from within. A light flickered. Shuffling footsteps. A bolt scraped, and the door opened. An old man stood holding a candle, peering out.

'What's up, Padgett; what d'ye want?' he croaked. Padgett nodded toward Jimmy.

'Brat to take to t'pit. Come and wind us down.'

The old man peered short-sightedly at Jimmy. 'Down t'pit: at this time o' night?' he said, incredulous. 'What for?'

Padgett made an impatient noise and groped in his pocket, bringing out a coin. This he pressed into the man's hand. 'Mr Rawdon's business, and not to be spoke of,' he whispered, conspiratorially. 'And now ger a move on.'

The old collier motioned to Padgett to step inside. He did so, dragging Jimmy with him. He never relaxed that iron grip. 'If he does,' thought Jimmy, panic stirring within him, 'I'm off; even with tied hands.' The prospect of being imprisoned in that hideous pit made him desperate. He waited his chance.

The old fellow went off to dress and Padgett pushed the boy down on to a stool. 'Sit there and 'old yer noise,' he said, and went over to a soft chair by the dying fire, where he sat, stirring up the coals with the heel of his boot. After a while the old man reappeared, and Padgett called to him. 'Come 'ere, Jacob: over 'ere where I can talk to ye.' Old Jacob shuffled across to Padgett's chair and bent down. Padgett began talking to him in a whisper. The grizzled head came between Padgett and his view of Jimmy. Jimmy saw and slid silently from his stool. It was difficult with his hands tied. He went on tiptoe across the stone-flagged floor toward the door. Only a single candle burned in the dimness of the room and the flickering shadows it cast covered his movement. He would have to lift the latch with his mouth. He flicked a glance towards the men, and bent his head to it. Leaning on the door with his shoulder to make the latch come up easily, he got the cold knob of iron between his teeth and lifted gently. His neck trembled with the tension. If he dropped the latch now, they would be upon him. It lifted smoothly out of its notch. He held it and took his shoulder from the door, very gradually. The door opened a crack, so that the latch was clear of the notch. Holding his breath, he began to lower it. His jaw trembled. His mouth tasted of rust. The latch was down. He put a foot against the door to keep it from swinging open, and straightened up. The wind blew drizzle through the crack on to his cheek. The old man was chuckling drily, turning. Now! He moved his foot and kicked the door wide, plunging out into the darkness. Across the road, stumbling in the ruts. A cry from the cottage. Shrubs crowded the road's edge. He bent his head and crashed through. Wet foliage lashed his face. Padgett blundered into the road, roaring, while Jimmy plunged on, stumbling between twisted stumps. He broke clear. A hayfield. Waist-high grasses, sodden, with bent heads. He waded in at a crouching run. Behind, Padgett was in the trees. Somewhere the old man called, cracked falsetto. In the middle of the field Jimmy threw himself down, wriggling desperately between the stalks: desperate to move, yet leave no trail. Hands. If only he had his hands.

Padgett, pausing at the field's rim, saw the flattened swathe and followed. The boy lay along the roots, cheek in spongy earth, and heard him, felt him coming. Swishing through the wet hay. He lay, mouth open, chest heaving. The rain soaked into his clothes; fell into his face. A trembling in the earth, a boot glistening by his face. Wriggle down. Merge with the earth. Melt into the rain. Give me back my hands, or make me earth, and grass, and rain.

He cried out as the great hand closed on his collar, jerking him erect. Cried out again as the other hand cracked into the side of his head; reeling, kicking, spitting, screaming: 'My hands: give me my hands!'

He fought, as best he could, all across the hayfield and through the trees.

He dug his heels into the ruts of the road, writhing and jerking. And all the time he cried out, crying to somebody, anybody, who might keep him from being sealed in hot narrow blackness for ever. He bit the hand that clawed to close his mouth so that, fearful lest better men should wake and see his deed, Padgett cudgelled him finally into oblivion.

9

JOE SAT at the foot of the hayrick, watching the sunset and nibbling the last of his bread. The stolen food had lasted him two days. The weather had stayed dry, too, and he was anxious to be on his way again. He had seen no sign of any pursuit. Still, he would wait until dark.

He took off his boots and examined them. There were large holes in both soles and the heels were almost worn away. He shrugged. His feet were hard from working barefoot in the pit, as he had often done. He put the boots on again and stood up, stretching. It had been a good place to spend the day, this hayrick. He would try to find another one, towards morning, when his night's walk was behind him.

He glanced toward the road. A farm cart was rumbling slowly along, the carter nodding over the reins. There was nothing else as far as he could see in either direction. He moved out of the hayrick's shadow and went quietly into the hedgerow, grinning to himself. The cart swayed along, the horse clop-clopping, head down, going at its own pace. When it had passed him Joe slipped out of the hedgerow and took hold of the cart's tail, swinging his feet on to the bar underneath. The carter continued to nod, and Joe kept one eye on him, across the load of turnips, and the other along the road. He rode thus for a good mile until, glancing behind, he saw a horseman. He jumped down and hid in the hedgerow until the rider came by. It was a farmer, going homeward at a steady trot. Still, thought Joe, the fewer people who saw him, the better. He lay in the hedge until it grew quite dark, before resuming his journey.

The moon hung round and full in the sky, and here where the trees overhung, the road was dappled with shadow-patterns of silver and black. Joe hurried along, peering fearfully into the gloom. Small sounds came to him: the comings and goings of night-creatures and the soughing of the wind in the tops. His footfalls seemed to echo, as though the night were a valley set all about with hills of darkness. He began to sing, softly, to the rhythm of his footfalls:

Early mornin', candles lit,
Along the road an' down the pit:
It's hard times in the pit, my dears,
Hard times in the pit.

The plaintive treble hung on the air and the wind carried it away like mist between the trees.

Ever hungry, oft-times sick,
Bend yer back an' swing yer pick . . .

He whirled glancing wildly all around as another voice, deep and resonant, came in upon the refrain:

> It's hard times in the pit, my dears,
> Hard times in the pit.

A rustle in the bracken, and a tall figure strode out upon the road. Joe backed away, gazing up into the grinning black-bearded face.

'Don't be afear'd.' The stranger's voice was gruff. 'I was a pit-brat once, myself.' Joe stopped backing away. The man towered over him, hands on hips. 'An' where might ye be heading for, at midnight an' all?'

Joe pointed along the road. 'Please, sir, I'm goin' to London: that way.'

The stranger laughed, swaying back on his heels. 'London, is it? To seek yer fortune, I'll be bound!' Joe shook his head.

'No, sir: to find a man.' A chuckle from the depths of the ragged beard.

'Aye, well: an' it's many a man ye'll be findin' in London: many a man!' And he chuckled again, his shoulders shaking. After a moment he said, 'What man are ye seekin'?' Joe shook his head and took another step backwards. He was determined to say no more. The man waited a moment, then shrugged good-naturedly.

'All right, young shaver: I'll not pry into yer business: though 'tis a fair piece yet to London, an' mebbe I can set ye on yer way a bit.' He bent down, eyeing Joe narrowly. 'From up around Bradford way, aren't ye?' Joe nodded. 'Runaway?' Joe nodded again. The man cocked his shaggy head on one side. 'Didn't *steal* nothin', did ye?' Joe shook his head.

'No, sir! Them notices was lies, sir. We never took nothin'.' The man straightened up, grinning broadly.

'Well; I don't know about no notices: but they puts up lyin' notices about *me*, too, so I gets yer drift!' He held out a huge hand toward the boy. 'Come on: I'll wager ye'd be better for a bite o' roast rabbit!'

Joe hesitated for only a moment. The stranger wore ragged clothes and the beard gave him a fierce aspect, but there was something about him that made Joe feel he could be trusted: he put out a small black hand.

The stranger strode rapidly between the trees, his hand wrapped around Joe's, so that the boy was obliged to trot through bracken as tall as himself. Some distance from the road they came to a clearing. There was a low shelter of boughs with a canvas thrown over it, and a smouldering fire. Over the fire a rough spit had been built and a rabbit sizzled softly in the smoke.

'Sit ye down, boy,' growled the man, nodding toward the fire. 'Get warm!' Joe sat, holding out his hands to the warmth. The stranger sat on the other side of the fire, taking the rabbit from the spit. He tore it into pieces with his great hands, gasping with the heat of it, and passed a chunk to Joe through the smoke. They sat awhile in silence, chewing fiercely and studying each other across the glow. Presently the stranger said: 'How long ye been on the road?'

'Three days, sir, I think.'

'Ye've done well, gettin' this far.' His eyes narrowed

again. 'Are they lookin' for ye?' Joe nodded. He decided not to mention the ten guineas reward. 'Ye said "we" a while back: "We never took nothing"; was there two of ye?'

Joe nodded again. 'My friend was took.'

He started, involuntarily, as the stranger said: 'Price on yer 'ead, is there?'

He could tell by the way it was said that there was no point in denying it. He nodded. 'Ten guineas.'

To his surprise the man laughed uproariously, rocking backwards and forwards and slapping his ragged knees with greasy hands. 'Ten guineas?' he spluttered. 'For the two of ye?' Joe nodded. When he had laughed his fill, the stranger said: 'Do ye know what price they put on *this* 'ead?' (Touching his matted hair.) Joe shook his head. 'Two 'undred guineas. Two 'undred!' The words echoed through the trees. Joe gasped.

'What did ye *do*?' he said, before he could stop himself. The man grinned.

'Do? Oh, I does a bit o' this an' a bit o' that: I moves around, like, livin' off them as can afford it!' He chuckled again, then leaned forward across the fire. 'I likes you,' he said, suddenly grave, ' 'ow'd ye like to *ride* a good piece of yer way?'

Joe was gazing open-mouthed at the stranger. A robber! He was sitting in the woods at midnight with a robber! Two hundred guineas! He had probably *killed* somebody to have that price on his head.

He gulped, and stammered: 'R—ride, sir: what d'ye mean, ride?' The man did not reply. He got to his feet and began to kick earth over the fire with the side of his boot. Joe stood up. When the fire was covered, the man stamped the earth down until there was only a little mound, from which a last wisp of smoke curled.

' 'Ere!' He bent, picking up the last of the rabbit, which he tossed to Joe. 'Eat this an' we'll be off!' He pulled the canvas from its frame of boughs. There was a bundle inside the shelter. He pulled this out, wrapping the canvas around it to make a roll. He strapped the roll across his shoulders and kicked over the framework of his shelter, scattering the boughs into the bracken. 'Two days,' he growled, 'an' nobody'll know we was ever 'ere.'

They went side by side, back toward the road. In the edge of the trees, the robber pulled Joe down into the bracken fronds. He pressed a finger to his lips and whispered, 'Quiet now: there'll be a carriage along soon, if I'm not mistook. Then we'll 'ave us a ride towards London!'

They lay for a while in the bracken. The road remained empty. The stranger had taken a pistol from his pocket and laid it near his hand. Joe gazed at its dull gleaming shape. His heart pounded. Perhaps he should not have stayed with this man. He was a thief: if they were taken they would both be transported; or hanged. Perhaps he should thank him for the rabbit, and say that he must be on his way now, because it was a long way that he had to go.

He looked at the man's face with the corner of his eye and was about to speak when a huge hand gripped his arm. 'Shush! Keep yer 'ead down until I calls ye!' The man's head was on one side in a listening attitude.

Far off, Joe heard the clop of hooves and the rattle of a vehicle.

The sounds drew nearer. The man raised himself into a crouch, the pistol in his great fist. 'Stay hid!' he hissed. 'Until I say!' The carriage came in sight, passing swiftly from light, to shadow, to light again. When it was almost opposite, the man sprang out upon the road, roaring, 'Hold! Hold there!' Joe saw the coachman jerk into abrupt wakefulness, hauling on the reins. Both horses reared, whickering and stamping to a halt, flinching in the harness. The coachman sat on the box, his arms raised above his head. The robber's pistol swung to the dark window. 'Any passengers?' he roared.

The coachman shook his head. 'I . . . I am taking the carriage to fetch my master from his club,' he stammered. 'He plays at cards.'

'I know,' growled the robber. 'I've watched you these five nights.'

The coachman looked terrified. 'Wh—what do you want with me?' he said. 'I have no valuables. There is nothing in the carriage.'

'I know that, too.' He glanced over his shoulder. 'Ye can come out now, boy,' he called. Joe rose to his feet. He was trembling violently, so that it was as much as he could do to walk into the road. The robber was grinning. He looked up at the coachman. ' 'Ave ye a weapon?'

'No, sir,' replied the coachman meekly.

'I'm comin' up beside ye,' said the robber. 'An' no tricks, mind, or I'll blow yer brains out an' leave ye in the ditch!' He opened the door of the carriage.

'Climb in, milord,' he said, bowing gravely, and lifting the boy into the dark interior.

Joe sat, dazed, in a shiny leather seat, as the thief clambered up to the box, shoving the coachman over none too gently. The coachman offered him the reins.

'You're the coachman,' growled the shaggy stranger. 'Drive! Straight through the town, an' show us some pace!' He pointed the pistol at the man's face. 'I couldn't miss you from 'ere,' he said, darkly.

The coachman, thankful still to have his life, whipped the horses into a gallop and the carriage swayed and bounced along the rutted road. They swept through the town, where the coachman's master sat at his cards, and out again into the dark countryside. Joe watched through the window as woods and rivers and villages flashed by, his eyes wide with the quickness of it. They drove until the first green streaks of dawn showed, away on their left side. Then, the pistol in his ribs, the coachman reined-in the lathered horses and the thief slipped down on to the road. He opened the door and handed Joe down. The boy blinked wearily in the dawn. His companion grinned.

'There's a good piece o' yer road behind ye now,' he growled. He glanced up at the coachman. 'Ye'd best go fetch yer master: 'e'll be weary o' the cards, likely, by the time ye get to 'im!'

The coachman watched dumbly as his strange passengers melted into the trees. Then he turned his carriage and urged the exhausted horses slowly northward up the long, rough road.

A little way into the wood the big man stopped and

grinned down at Joe. 'Well, young feller,' he smiled. 'That's yer way now.' He pointed. 'Yonder's Bedford. 'Twould be best to wait for night before goin' through. I'm off this way.' He pointed west. 'To try my luck at Worcester: long time since I was at Worcester!' He held out a hand, and they shook, solemnly. 'Good luck to ye, in London,' he growled.

Joe looked into the fierce face, that had so much kindness behind it. 'Good luck to ye, at Worcester,' he whispered. He felt as though there might be tears in his eyes, so he turned abruptly and walked a few steps into the trees, and when he looked round the robber was gone.

10

'Do not struggle, boy, or you'll have the roof down!' Jimmy stopped pulling on the thick chain and screwed his eyes toward the dim figure that lay, propped on one elbow, a few feet away. The figure raised its shaggy head and spoke again. 'They've fastened our chains round props, so that if we attempt to loosen them, we shall be buried alive.'

Even in the almost total darkness Jimmy could see that this was true. His own chain had been fastened to one leg-iron, passed around a rotten-looking prop, and then secured to his other ankle. The irons bit into

the flesh, but at least his hands were free at last. He looked towards his fellow captive.

'How long have you been here, sir?' he asked. The other's shrug was lost in the darkness.

'I do not know, exactly. What is today's date?' Jimmy shook his head slowly.

'I don't rightly know, sir: sometime in September, I think.'

The man was silent for a moment. 'Then it is seven months, very near, since I was brought here,' he said wearily.

Jimmy gasped. 'Seven months! But why, sir: who *are* you?' Why do they keep you here?' For a time, there was no reply. Water was dripping somewhere and the chains clinked softly from time to time.

Finally, the man began to speak, slowly, as though very tired.

'My name is Croft. I am the brother of Joseph Croft. Since you were in the workhouse here, I have no doubt that you have heard of him. You may also have heard that his brother disappeared some time ago, taking with him almost the entire family fortune!' He paused, peering intently at the boy through the darkness. It seemed to Jimmy that some response was expected.

'Yes, sir: I . . . I have heard tell of this: paupers talking . . .'

'Quite. A story put about by Rawdon, and those in his employ, to discredit the name of Croft and to hide his own guilt.' The weak voice broke off in a fit of coughing, then continued, hoarsely. 'I tell you all this, you understand, because your plight is connected directly with my own. There is certain information which Rawdon requires of me, and which I will not divulge. You have been placed here as a further inducement to me to tell him what he wants to know. I am told that you will receive no food until I speak.' A short pause, then: 'Nevertheless I will tell them nothing, and for that I must beg your pardon.'

The boy nodded, dumbly. He understood now why they had questioned him; why he had been beaten. 'It's the money, sir, isn't it?'

Croft nodded. 'Yes: the money with which my brother means to found a school: a school of industries.' The weak voice became contemplative. 'It will be the first of its kind: a place where the children of the poor will come to learn to read and write, and be taught a trade: so that one day, perhaps, there might *be* no more poor.' Again, that harsh cough, echoing away down the blackness: 'The first of its kind, but not the last,' he croaked. 'Not the last.'

A long silence, broken only by the wheezing of the

sick man's breath. Jimmy understood only a part of what Croft had told him. It was true, then, that Mr Croft was concerned for pit-brats: if only he had been there when he and Joe had sought him. Joe! Where was Joe now? Taken, more than likely; or dead. And now this: to die of hunger here in the dark. Or to struggle, and so die more quickly when the roof came in. His frightened thoughts were interrupted by Croft, who seemed now to be rambling. 'The money was at the house: in gold. All those pictures sold; all that silver; the horses. . . . Work was to begin: timber was being cleared in preparation for building.'

The voice was so thin now, so faint, that Jimmy had to strain to catch the words: the blackness seemed to muffle them. 'A man came to the house. A collier named Fawcett: his brother works here still, I believe: perhaps you have heard of him? Anyway, he came to see my brother. Joseph was in London and the man saw me. He told me that some colliers would come by night to take away the money. It was to be that same night. I told the man to bring the constable, and he went, only to return after a few minutes to say that the colliers were in the grounds. I let the dogs out and the fellow helped me to fasten up the gold in two bags. We carried it outside. The dogs were making a great noise: there was some shouting, and a shot. The bags were heavy, but we got them away to . . .' Here he paused, uncertainly. 'To a place of safety. We were on the road back when they came at us from the hedge. They had cudgels.' Another fit of coughing: the man's fetters rattled with every spasm. Presently he continued. 'I came to, to find myself here. They told me the collier was dead and that I would be dead also, very soon. Then the questioning began. They beat me, starved me, and left me alone for days on end. I knew that once Rawdon had the money he would kill me. At first I thought he might kill me anyway, since he was interested only in stopping our school of industries: with me dead, the money would lie hidden for ever, and so his purpose would be accomplished. But gradually he became more and more concerned with the money for its own sake, so that now his original purpose is lost to him: he will have that gold, at whatever cost. But he shall not . . . he shall not!'

The coughing this time was so severe, the frail body so racked, that when it was over Croft lay gasping on the damp floor, too weakened even to lift his head. He remained so for a long time, and Jimmy half-sat, propped against the wall, pondering all that he had heard. Presently the man's fetters rattled as he struggled into a sitting position.

'Tell me,' he croaked thinly. 'What became of the other child: the small one who came to me here?'

Jimmy sighed. 'He wasn't taken with me, sir: he was running into a wood, the last time I saw him. But London's a long way, sir, and I think him taken by now, or dead.'

'Not taken with you!' It was almost a shout. 'They didn't tell me *that*! They said they were bringing me some company, and so my last hope was gone!'

'There's no hope, sir,' said Jimmy tiredly. 'He's such a small boy, sir: he'd never reach London alone.'

'It is wrong to think as you do,' said Croft softly. 'I have gone on hoping, because those like Rawdon do not prosper, in the end. You will see: what my brother wants to do is *right*, and so it will be accomplished.' He shifted his position, lying down along the floor. 'Sleep now, boy, for they will come at dawn to cover our mouths, so that we cannot call out.'

Jimmy lay down, cradling his head in his arms. He was stiff from the beating and his head ached. The words of the poor sick man who lay near by had not cheered him: the long months of darkness must have unhinged him, so that now he might believe anything. Jimmy felt a tightness in his throat. Darkness and the sense of hopelessness overwhelmed him, so that he wept quietly there, deep in the earth until weariness overtook him too; and he slept in spite of all this, but on a sleeve sodden with tears.

II

THE THIN COLLIER set down his beer-mug and leaned a little, casting an ear towards the talk at the next table. Three farmhands, crouched solidly over the scarred oak, thick red hands wrapped around pewter mugs. The tavern was noisy and the words came to him indistinctly through the din. 'Aye, an' 'e's just nicely set out to fetch 'is master 'ome, when a great fellow jumps out o' the trees with a pistol in 'is 'and. "Pull up," says 'e. "Me an' this young lad'll ride a way with ye." ' The speaker paused, gazing into the square, ruddy faces of his companions as though assessing the effect of his story. Their raised eyebrows and grunts of interest seemed to satisfy him, for he continued, as the pale collier leaned nearer: 'Slap in middle o' Buck wood, it were. Coachman reckons the brat were a pit-boy or a climbin' boy or summat: black all over an' hunched a bit about the shoulders. Anyway, they gets up, an' old coachman 'as to drive all night at the gallop, near clear to Bedford, afore they'll get down.'

The man lifted his mug and took a long pull, while his cronies watched him. He wiped his mouth with the back of his hand and said: 'Then the big feller gets down, 'ands the kid out o' the coach, an' they runs off into the trees. Coachman 'as to stop to rest the 'orses, an' 'tis night-time afore 'e gets back to Manor 'ouse. 'E says both 'orses is broken-winded an' fit for nothing now; an' 'is master's proclaimed twenty guineas reward for the man that brings in either o' the scoundrels: if I were free to go, I'd be after 'em myself.'

The collier drained his mug and rose, throwing a coin on the table. He paused by the three labourers, bending. 'What town was that, where the robbers got down?' he said. The men looked up at him. ''Twere Bedford, if it's owt to ye,' said the narrator coldly. 'Weren't talkin' to you anyhow,' he added to the retreating back.

Bedford. Joe stood on the hill and gazed at the town below. He had never heard the name, but the man had said it was a good piece of his road gone; and they *had* come far and fast, in that gleaming coach. A coach! Trapper Joe, eater of good farmhouse vittles and rider in fast coaches! He grinned, and slipped off the road to bypass the town. He went silently between the trees in a great half-circle that brought him, a little after midday, near to the road again, beyond Bedford. Here he lay up in a bramble thicket, listening to the carts and the riders and the laughing farmhands who passed unknowing within a few yards of his hiding-place. For a time he slept, and while he slept a cart went by with a pale thin passenger, who scanned with narrowed eyes the rolling road and the fields at either side.

He awoke in the dusk. The road was loud with workers going homeward. He lay looking at the sky through the tangle. He was hungry again. When it was quiet, and almost dark, he got up, brushing the dead leaves from his ragged jacket. In the pocket he found some stale crumbs which he put into his mouth. They made him feel more hungry. His earlier high spirits seemed to have dissolved, and it was a downcast figure that emerged on to the road and shuffled south.

Presently he came round a bend and found himself looking into a village. Low cottages on both sides of the road, with lighted windows. He dropped into the ditch, ankle-deep in water, and peered carefully between the grass-stems. The road curved through the village, and on the other side, some distance away, stood an inn. A coach stood in front of the inn and passengers were getting down and going inside. A smell of cooking came to Joe on the wind. He groaned, feeling his hunger.

He waited until the inn yard was silent and nobody was to be seen on the street. Then he scrambled out of the ditch and went silently into the village; creeping past cottage doors and dodging in and out of shadows, until he came opposite the inn. The smell of food made him ravenous, and he could see a woman passing back and forth behind the yellow windows, carrying trays with platters and mugs. He crossed the road, skirting the square of latticed-light thrown upon it, and peered into the yard. The coach stood horseless on the cobbles. Beyond it the stable doors stood blackly open. A smell of fresh hay and of tired horses mingled with the food smell. A door opened and a man stood silhouetted in it, holding a platter. He called out, 'Sam! Sam: come take yer supper now!' Joe drew back. Another figure emerged from the stables. A boy, about his own height. The boy took the platter and walked back into the stable. The man waited until he was inside, then went in and closed the door.

Joe's mouth watered. Hunger made him forget his caution. He slipped into the yard and walked on his toes to the stable door. A faint glow came from somewhere within. A rhythmic sound, like a razor on a strop. He went in, tiptoeing on straw between dark stalls where dim shapes moved restlessly, now and then whickering softly. The stalls ended. Joe caught his breath and stopped. On the floor sat the boy, his back against a stack of hay. A lantern stood before him and by its light the boy was rubbing something into the leather of a saddle which lay between his knees. Among the straw by the lad's elbow sat the platter, with bread and cheese and an onion. He was whistling softly as he worked. Suddenly he looked up. Joe pulled back sharply into the shadow and his head struck a beam. He grunted sharply and the boy came to his feet, lifting the lantern. 'Who . . . who's there?' he piped tremulously. 'What do you want?'

Joe made a swift decision and stepped forward into the light. 'I'm called Joe,' he said, 'I want summat to eat.'

The other boy took a step to the rear, peering round the lantern. 'There's something on the floor there.' The boy touched the platter with his bare foot. 'You can have that, if you want.' He stepped back again as the black figure advanced, crouching to the food. Joe knelt, stuffing the food into his mouth, tearing it with his fingers; watching the lantern. The boy stared at him. 'Where you from?'

'Long way,' grunted Joe through the food.

'When you've eaten that you'll have to go: Ned'll be back in a minute.'

'I'll go now: I'm takin' the rest o' this with me.' Joe scooped up the remains of the food, pushing it into his pocket. He began to back away. 'Not a word, mind, till I'm gone!' he whispered. The boy shook his head emphatically.

Joe was halfway toward the door when he heard footfalls in the yard. He ran back to the boy. 'Any other way out?' The boy shook his head again.

'No: you'll have to hide. I won't give you away.' He pointed to the stack of hay. 'Squeeze in behind there. An' keep quiet, mind!'

Joe crabbed swiftly into the space between the hay and the rough wall. The gap was narrow and the hay rustled with the slightest move. He froze.

'Hey, Sam! You finished that saddle yet?'

'Nearly, Ned. I been eating my supper.'

'Made short work of it, too, by the look of it. Better get back to that saddle quick.'

Joe held his breath. How long would it be before the man called Ned moved away a little? It was almost impossible to remain absolutely still in this position. The boy spoke again: 'Hey, Ned: I think you ought to take a look at one of them horses that came in with the coach just now: the dapple mare. She's lame, I reckon.'

'Oh, aye? Well, ye'd best show me then, young Sam.'

Joe's heart warmed to his young ally. He listened to the receding footfalls. They were carrying the lantern away. He waited a moment, then edged rapidly from behind the hay. He glanced around. Lantern-light revealed two figures in a distant stall, bending. He tiptoed quickly to the door and took to his heels across the yard. He was opposite the side door when it opened. The light fell full upon him. The same man was standing there. 'Hey! Hey you, boy!' he yelled, clattering out on to the cobbles. 'Stop! What you up to, eh?' Joe swerved past him and reached the gate. 'Help!' cried the man. 'Help! Thief! Thief!' Joe was out upon the road, pelting south along the street. The inn door was flung open as he passed it. Voices behind him, querulous: 'Hey, ostler; what's the rub?' and 'Thief? Where-away?'

He threw a glance over his shoulder. A knot of figures in the doorway, pointing, shouting. He put his head down and raced on around the curve. Nobody followed. He slowed to a jog, looking back. Nobody. The cottages were thinning out. He passed the last of them and stopped, panting, listening for hoofbeats. Had no gentleman saddled up to pursue? Nothing. Distant voices. He walked on the road's edge, trees close on his right hand. Still listening. After a while he fished the onion from his pocket and bit into it, savagely; grinning as he limped along.

They refilled the ostler's mug. He sat in the ingle, basking in firelight and attention. 'What did the fellow look like?' somebody asked.

'Oh: great lout of a feller,' said the ostler, bravely. 'I nearly 'ad 'im, though, for all that!'

A gentleman in a plum weskit turned aside to hide his smile. 'A decidedly small fellow, or my eyes play me false,' he murmured to himself. The ostler took a pull on his ale. A thin, rough-looking man pushed through the buzzing throng whose dull evening had been so unexpectedly enlivened.

'What d'ye say 'e looked like?' he asked eagerly. 'Was 'e ragged, like, an' black-dirty?'

'Aye: ragged; an' as black-dirty as I ever saw.'

'An' was 'e about this 'igh?' The thin man stooped, levelling a grimy palm about four feet above the floor. The ostler looked insulted.

'Indeed 'e were *not*,' he spluttered. ''E were fourteen 'ands if 'e were an inch!'

The gentleman in the plum weskit guffawed over

his tankard. 'Come now,' he boomed. 'He was as high as this fellow indicated, and no higher: a child, or I'm a tinker's dog!' The ostler flushed.

'I beg your pardon, sir, but yer mistaken. 'E were 'igher than me, sir; and savage-lookin'.'

'A child!' the gentleman insisted. 'An urchin. But come, let me fill your mug again: your yarn relieves the tedium!'

The travellers laughed good-humouredly, drifting from the ingle. The outer door opened briefly and slammed. The thin man was no longer present.

All night Joe trudged steadily south. The food made a warm glow inside him, and he felt happy. London was not far now. How many days would it have been before he came here, if it had not been for the kindly thief? He stopped, once, to kick off the tattered boots which had become a hindrance to him, and whistled through his teeth as he went on barefoot.

At dawn he found a hayrick in a field near Stevenage and slept there throughout the day. He would have slept less soundly had he known that, around midday, a thin man sat down nearby to remove his boots and rub his throbbing feet. After a while the man put on his boots and begged a ride on a haycart going towards Barnet.

When Joe awoke at twilight he felt hot and his head ached. He looked out. It was raining. A spiteful wind hissed round the rick, whipping out loose straws and plastering them on the hedge. When he breathed in his throat burned. He wanted to stay where he was and go to sleep again: but the end of his journey was so near now. He had to go on. He thought of Jimmy and the man in closed road, and hauled his aching body out of the warm hay.

Within minutes the rain was through to his skin and a violent shivering set in. His teeth chattered uncontrollably. He hunched his head into the upturned collar of his jacket and plunged on numbly, his naked feet splashing through puddles and ankle-deep mud. He was dizzy and confused and, when a coach came up fast from behind, the plunging, steaming horses were almost on him before he flung himself sideways into the ditch. A startled cry from the coachman, a rumble and splash, and it was gone, swaying off into the wet blackness. Joe lay in the sodden grass, shuddering. When he tried to rise, his legs would not support him. He went on hands and knees for a while in the edge of the road, racked with sickness. The rain beat down on his thin back and the wind cut him to the bone. The ground seemed to move under him, whirling endlessly past his burning eyes until, with a shuddering moan, he toppled sideways and lay still.

Towards morning the wind died and the rain stopped. The moon slid down the sky between rags of cloud that drifted slowly westward, and the east was tinged with pink. The huddled figure moved a little in the roadside.

Joe opened his eyes. His mouth had mud in it. He raised his head, spluttering. A wave of giddiness washed over him so that he lowered his leaden head again into the pale mud. After a while he moved again, hauling his numb body into a sitting position.

He closed his eyes against the spinning road, retching. When the spasm passed he opened his eyes, looking round vaguely. A sound, somewhere behind the pounding in his head. There: a way off yet, but coming on. A horse. He dragged himself to the verge; sliding down the turf into the black ditch, peering with burning eyes over the rim. In the half-light came a shaggy pony pulling a caravan. The old man at the reins seemed to be dozing. Joe waited, trying to stop the shaking in his limbs. He could not think. London. The caravan: was it going the right way? He tried to remember. It didn't matter. It was nearly here now. He clawed up the bank, tottered to his feet. The pony saw, flinching a little. The old man's head stayed down. Joe dragged his feet toward the slow vehicle. The big wheels ground by, splashing his naked toes. He stared down at his toes, frowning. Wool inside his head. The caravan was past.

He gazed after it; gave a little cry and ran, arms outstretched, after the bouncing tailboard. His clawing fingers found a hold and he dragged his feet clear of the mud, kicking weakly to find the bar underneath. In his dizziness he almost lost his grip but his feet found the bar. He pushed himself up until he could hook one elbow over the tailboard. He looked blankly into the dim interior. Nobody. Bundles of some kind. He might ride inside. Pushing with his feet, straining his arms, he was unable to lift himself. He sagged back again, fighting sickness, and allowed himself to hang limply; each jolt threatening to tear free his tenuous hold.

The sky became lighter. The caravan began to pass

labourers on their way to the fields. Joe's grip on the tailboard was instinctive now: in his dream he floated at peace through a place of silver mist; rising and falling as though on a softly roaring tide. Daylight flooded the countryside, and now and then a walker would turn in his track to stare at the limp, ragged figure that hung as though crucified behind the van; but no one called out, nor came nearer to see.

The sun rose out of misty fields, burning sullenly. The old man grunted, blinked, and roused himself. Barnet. Today he was to sell his wares at Barnet. He looked at the sun, and muttered an oath. He was late; he had slept and this idle beast had taken its time. He snapped the reins, roaring. The pony lunged forward. The caravan lurched violently and Joe's hold was loosed. He fell like a rag doll into the road and lay still.

He was in a hayrick now: a warm, dry, sweet-smelling hayrick. He had all the time in the world: he had nowhere to go, and nobody was looking for him. He was free. He wriggled down luxuriously into the sweet, springy hay. Somewhere, very far away, a voice was calling. He smiled lazily and opened his eyes a little. The hayrick went away. Something slammed into his side. A tall thin man looked down at him. The voice again, very close this time.

'Hello, Trapper,' it said.

12

PADGETT RODE the clatch-iron up into the starry night. Rawdon paced by the headgear, impatient. 'Well?'

Padgett let the clatch go, shaking his head. ' 'E's sayin' nowt, as usual.'

'You didn't leave the food?'

'No. It's 'ere.' He patted his pocket.

Rawdon went over to the man who stood by the winding-gear. 'Here: take this. We'll not be needing you again tonight.' The collier took the coin, turning away. 'See that you guard your tongue when you spend that in the Duke,' said Rawdon.

'You can trust me, sir.' He shambled off toward the town.

Rawdon and Padgett watched him go. Padgett looked uneasy. 'Too many of 'em know summat now, I reckon,' he said. 'It's goin' to get out, sir, one o' these days.'

Rawdon made an impatient gesture. 'You do as you're told, Padgett,' he growled. 'That's what I pay you for.'

They walked slowly towards the road. 'I'm worried about that brat, sir: that trapper. 'E's not took yet; could be 'e's nearin' London by this.'

'I have men all over London,' said Rawdon. 'And

others on the roads to London. Nobody could get past all of them. The brat is probably lying dead somewhere at this moment.'

'It's takin' too long: I don't reckon they'll ever talk, sir. I say get rid of 'em'. Rawdon turned, thrusting his florid face into the collier's. '*I* will decide what is best, Padgett!' he roared. 'I am capable of such decision, and you are not: that is why you are a collier, while I am an owner!' He spluttered, incoherent with rage. 'There is a fortune in gold hidden somewhere near here, and if you think a . . . a brat is going to cheat me of it, then you are a bigger fool even than I took you for!'

Padgett made no reply, but his uneasiness was in no way lessened. He regarded his enraged master sidelong as they trudged up the road. With the gold hidden, and Croft dead, the School of Industries could never be built. Wasn't that what mattered? It seemed to him that his master was risking everything for the sake of the gold. He sighed softly in the dark. When a man has one fortune, what does he want with two?

They came to the gates of Rawdon House. Rawdon paused in the driveway. 'There's a great deal at stake here, Padgett,' he said, in more reasonable tones. 'They'll talk, sooner than die; and when they do, you will have reason to be glad that you were loyal to me.'

They parted. Padgett clumped down into the town and, plagued by his uneasy thoughts, turned in to the tavern, shouting for ale. Presently he smiled over his tankard, his fingers sifting the gold that jingled in his pocket. It was not every collier who had tavern-gold for the asking. Perhaps Rawdon was right, there was nothing to worry about. And if something went wrong? Well, Mr Rawdon would find a way out; he always did.

13

THE BOOT came swinging again and Joe rolled to avoid it. 'On yer feet!' snarled the thin collier. Joe screwed up his eyes and shook his head. He felt sick and weak. His head ached dully. The realisation that it was over spread slowly through the hot fog of his mind, so that tears stood in his eyes as he scrambled shakily to his feet. 'Quit yer blubberin'! hissed the man. 'Ye'll walk wi' me as master an' boy: an' no tricks. Ye've led us a merry enough chase as it is.' He nodded south and gave the boy a heavy push. Joe reeled, almost falling, and shuffled along the road, his feet dragging. The collier trudged beside and a little behind him.

Afterwards, Joe could remember little of that long hot walk: just the endless road unwinding before him, and the collier trudging behind. They passed through Barnet. It was a market day and there were a lot of people about, but nobody paid any heed to the pale thin child, shuffling unhappily beside his grim master. It was a common enough sight. From time to time, the collier would move in close, thrusting his mouth at Joe's ear to remind him to be silent. They came again into open country, pressing on towards London. Once, the collier stopped a man to ask the hour: when he knew it, he gave Joe another push, snarling, 'Move! We can meet 'em before dark.' Whom they were to meet Joe did not know and had not the heart to ask.

The sun moved down the sky. As afternoon gave way to evening, Joe's fever subsided and he became more aware of his surroundings. They were entering London, moving through streets of small shops and many taverns. The collier began asking directions of people they met. Joe wondered why they were going on to London. Why was he not being taken back to Rawdon Pit, as he had expected? He looked at the collier out of the corner of his eye and said, 'Where ye takin' me?'

The man glanced at him sharply. 'Strand: didn't ye 'ear me ask?'

'What's Strand?'

'Where we meet t'others to tell 'em you're took.'

'T'others?'

'Aye: Mr Rawdon's 'ad a pitful o' men seekin' thee: an' 'e'll make ye pay for it, an' all, when 'e gets 'is 'ands on ye!'

They went on for a time in silence. Presently the man accosted an old woman as dusk began to fall. 'Strand?' she croaked, turning to point. 'That there's Villiers Street. Keep straight on and ye'll come to a silversmith's shop: Drury's. It's on the corner of the Strand.'

As he stumbled along, Joe noticed many alleyways leading off both sides of the street. It was almost dark now. If he could make a run: if he once got into one of those alleys . . . His mind was clearing rapidly. Soon they would meet with this man's friends. Rawdon's men: and it would be all up with him. He had little doubt about what would become of him once he was back in Rawdon's power. If he was going to escape then it must be *now*: somewhere in this city was the man he had come to find. Had he got so far, and come so close, only to be dragged away again? He looked up. Here was the corner. There, across the road, the silversmith's shop. The collier prodded him, crossing towards the shop. A gaslight burned within. The display of dishes and candelabra in the window reflected the pale yellow glow. Joe's heart hammered. Now? No; for the man suddenly grabbed his arm and bending close, whispered: 'Not a sound, mind, inside 'ere!' He was dragged into the shop. A man was packing something into a drawer. He turned, startled, as the unkempt pair appeared.

'Y—yes? What can I do for you?' he asked in a thin voice.

'I'm lookin' for Manchester 'ouse,' growled the collier. 'Manchester 'ouse, in the Strand.'

The silversmith came round the counter, hesitatingly, as though expecting to be attacked. 'Ah yes: yes; that is just across the way. If it were daylight, you would be able to read the name on the wall.' He was pointing. The finger trembled a little. 'There: where the windows are lighted on the first floor.' The collier was bending; following the direction of the finger. Joe glanced round. It must be now! The man still held his arm, but loosely as he peered between the piled silverware. On the counter stood a tall candlestick. Joe lunged, grabbing it, swinging wildly. The collier yelled, straightening up, and the candlestick's heavy base hit him on the head. He staggered, arms flailing. Joe, terrified, swung again. The collier fell to his knees. The silversmith backed up to his counter, screeching wildly for help. The collier toppled forward, crumpling to the floor. The silversmith ran for the door, crying out: 'Murder! Help! Help!' Joe stood an instant petrified, the candlestick loose in his hand. He looked to the door. The silversmith was in the street. Others were coming. Shouts. He lowered his head and ran, scattering the knot of people; butting through, making for the nearest alley. Footsteps pounded after him. Cries of 'Murder!' and 'Stop him!' A man came at him. He dodged away, cut off from the alley; ran down the street, tiring. The cries were bringing others; some in front. Four men, strung out across the street, arms out to catch him. He whirled, seeking a direction. They were behind and before him. To one side, an open-fronted shop, dark inside. He ran, leaping up the single step on to the straw-strewn planks. A dairy: pails on a counter and at the back, stalls with tethered cows. He vaulted the stalls. The cows scattered, lowing. His pursuers crashed into the shop. He leapt up the limewashed wall, scrabbling for the single small window, fell back. Leapt again. Strong hands grabbed him, hauling him back. Shouts. Men, pressing in. Blows. He struggled, borne down under the weight of his captors: lay on the planks, arms wrapped round his head. They pressed in, crying out: 'Kill 'im: Do 'im in, the murderer!'

A new voice, raucous, authoritative. 'No one's dead: stand back there; stand clear!' The press fell back to admit the newcomers. Joe opened his eyes. Two constables. 'Come on, young 'un, get up!' He rose, tottering. One of them took his arm, steadying him. He was faint with terror. The silversmith was shouting at the other constable, gesticulating. People in the crowd still cried for his blood. After a while they fell back, reluctantly, and he was taken between the two policemen into the dark street.

In the crowd stood two men very like the collier who lay senseless on the silversmith's floor. They watched as the child was led off.

'Well, that's it, then.'

'Aye: we can get back now, I reckon.'

'D'ye think Rawdon'll be satisfied?'

The other nodded towards the three retreating figures. 'Saves 'im a job, don't it?'

'What'll the brat get?'

'Armed robbery: 'e'll get the drop.'

'Armed?'

'Candlestick: pinched it, an' all.'

The crowd was dispersing. Drizzle fell thinly, misting the gaslights. The two men turned, hunching their shoulders, and clumped away along the gleaming cobbles.

14

THE CAB rattled to a halt. Joseph Croft paid the cabby and stepped down. The morning was damp, blustery. His eyes followed the black hansom as it faded slowly to grey, then he turned and strode across the pavement, mounted steps two at a time and struck the dull brass knocker.

The door was opened by Grey's manservant who said that his master was not yet risen, and would he care to wait? He was shown into a familiar room, and the manservant went away.

Croft stood with his hands clasped behind him

and looked out upon the street through a rain-beaded window. It was a broad street in a fashionable part of London. The houses were handsome and dignified, with ornate railings, pillared entrances and well-proportioned, many-paned windows. It was in this area that most of Croft's allies dwelt: men of influence who shared, besides wealth and position, an awareness of the many injustices that existed in the grimy world outside their own polite and comfortable circle. There was a movement afoot to end the worst of these injustices; a movement which was growing in strength and in resolution. Yet the forces ranged against it were stronger and if anything more resolute. There were men, rich and powerful men, who believed that to release the children from the factories and mines would be to ruin the economy of the country: would bring about the collapse of those industries upon which Britain was building an empire. And allied with these mistaken yet sincere men were others whose personal fortunes would certainly suffer if the working children were taken from their employ. Many were the battles being fought between these two mighty forces, in parliament, on the debating platform and in dingy common meeting-rooms everywhere. And so far, as Croft was only too grimly aware, the forces of reform had come off worst in these encounters: it was always a harder task to change things than to defend an existing situation.

He sighed, turning from the window. The task had lately become harder for him personally, too. Most people believed that his brother had deserted the cause; taking with him the Croft fortune so that it might not be used in the struggle. He himself refused to believe any such thing, though months had passed and no word had come as to his brother's fate. The incident had provided welcome ammunition for the enemies of the movement and they had seized upon it, using it to sway those who were undecided as to which side to support. Even some of his friends had cooled a little, since he appeared to them to be the brother of an unprincipled rascal. And since he now found himself virtually without fortune, his own contribution was perforce confined to making speeches.

The door opened and Grey strode in smiling. 'Croft! An early bird, and none the less welcome for that!' Croft took the extended hand and they shook warmly.

'There's a great deal to be done, Grey,' replied Croft. 'Therefore, the earlier the better!'

Grey patted his stomach and grimaced in mock agony. 'A man works badly on an empty belly, Croft; and more badly for being roused in the middle of the night!'

Croft smiled, nodding towards the clock on the mantel. 'As you can see, 'tis nine-thirty of a September morning, and honest men have been astir these three hours!'

'Then Lord spare me the ways of honest men!' said Grey with feeling. He became serious. 'How can I help you, Croft?'

'You will be going into the House this morning?' Grey nodded affirmation.

Croft said, 'There will be an attempt to persuade the Government to set up a Commission: we would welcome your support in this attempt.'

'A Commission?'

'A Parliamentary Commission to look into the conditions of child labourers and to report in detail to Parliament.'

Grey stood warming his back at the hearth. 'An ambitious undertaking. Naturally it shall have my support.' He seemed to recall something, for he snapped his fingers, crying, 'Your particular interest is in mining-children, I know.'

He had the air of one who has a good story to tell.

'It is,' said Croft. 'Why?'

'Oh: something Sambrook was telling me last evening: Sambrook, my valet. It quite slipped my mind; can't think why.'

Croft waited, impatient. 'Well?' he said.

'Sambrook is an incorrigible gossip,' said Grey, refusing to be hurried. 'And, in his free time, a frequenter of low establishments in undesirable quarters of the city. Many are the horrid tales he picks up there, with which to regale me while laying out my things!' He paused again, savouring his friend's curiosity. 'Well; it seems that last evening the whole city was buzzing with stories of a somewhat unusual armed robbery which was committed the previous evening at the Strand. According to Sambrook, a man was beaten almost to death with a silver candlestick.' Another pause.

Croft said, 'That does not sound especially unusual.'

'Ah!' said Grey, wagging a finger. 'But wait: there is more!' He took out a silk handkerchief, delicately dabbing at his nose, before continuing. 'The deed was done by a child, and the child was a pit-brat from

somewhere in the north: apparently he had *walked* to London.' He noted with satisfaction the light of interest in Croft's face. He continued, with relish: 'When the child was hauled up before a magistrate yesterday he babbled some cock-and-bull story about having come to London to seek a gentleman: had a message for him, but declined to impart it to the magistrate, even when it was pointed out to him that his neck might be forfeit!' Grey folded the handkerchief meticulously and dropped it into his pocket. 'No: he would not reveal his message, but he produced an old brass button and said the gentleman would know if he saw that!' Grey, who had been smiling faintly with his last words looked up startled as Croft strode across the room, plainly agitated.

'A button, you say? What kind of button: what did it look like?'

'My dear fellow, I have no idea!' Grey's voice sounded pained. 'It is simply a tale of Sambrook's: might be quite untrue, for all I know.'

'Ring for Sambrook!' cried Croft. 'I must speak to him!'

Grey seemed suddenly to realise that something was seriously upsetting his guest. 'Yes: very well. But *do* sit down, old fellow, you look most unwell: *most* unwell!'

Sambrook was summoned, but was unable to add anything to the tale as told by his master. 'My friend never 'eard the gentleman's name, sir, because the kid never said it,' he explained.

'Was your friend actually in court?' snapped Croft. He was pacing the room.

'Oh yes, sir: 'e goes whenever there's anything out of the ordinary, sir; for the entertainment, like.'

'Quite. And can you take me to where the child is being held now?'

'Why yes, sir: 'e's 'eld at Newgate awaitin' trial, sir.'

Croft turned to Grey. 'May I take this man for an hour?'

Grey was stunned by this turn of events. He said, 'There's no need: I will accompany you myself. Has the child some connection with *you*?' The tone was incredulous.

'I don't know!' snapped Croft, impatient. 'But it is possible: by God, it is possible!'

15

JOE HUDDLED in his corner, hugging his knees, and gazing morosely across the cell. It was a long cell, with dirty straw on its stone floor. Five others shared it with him. He was chained to the wall by one ankle, and four of the other five were chained also. One prisoner was unfettered: a gentle, shambling fellow who spent his time gazing through the bars, crooning to himself, and who passed his companions' pannikins out to the turnkey at mealtimes.

Nearest to Joe lay a thin youth with a bitter, cynical expression. It was with this youth that Joe had mostly spoken since being brought here the previous day.

'Naw; you ain't likely to get off wiv less than 'angin',' the youth had told him. 'I've seen 'em come an' I've seen 'em go; an' them as goes armed is always stretched.' This had only served to confirm what Joe already knew. He was finished. He had used the candlestick as a weapon: he had taken it with him when he ran in panic from the shop. If he had run after the *first* blow; if he had dropped the candlestick, he might have been away through the alleyways before the silversmith raised the hue and cry. Inside himself he knew, dimly, why he had waited to strike twice at the thin collier. Something had welled up in him: something like the feeling that he had felt when he stood in that twilit field with his stolen food; but stronger, darker. A kind of dark exultation that rose up to deny that he was only a trapper, and therefore nothing. When he swung that candlestick, it seemed to him that he was real; something to be reckoned with.

And now the illusion had gone. He was a small boy chained to a wall, whom they would hang, and consider the world well rid of another incorrigible young animal. He was nothing to them: nothing to anybody. He moved his hand to his pocket, forgetting momentarily that they had taken the button away from him. He had not even that, now. He felt the tears start in his eyes, and rubbed them quickly with grubby knuckles. The cynical youth had seen.

'Don't blubber, young 'un!' he called sarcastically. 'I'll remember yer, if ye like, when I'm at Bot'ny Bay!'

Anger swept through Joe. He was about to choke out some bitter retort, which would have served only to amuse the youth further, when a turnkey came along the dim passage and unlocked the iron door. He came across to Joe, wrinkling his nose at the stench in the cell. 'Come on, you: someone to see you.' His leg-iron was loosed, and the turnkey marched him out, holding him by the collar. Cries of 'Good luck, young 'un!' and 'Tell 'em you wasn't there!' came from the cells on both sides as they went along the passage.

They came to a solid door. The turnkey opened it and pushed Joe through. He stood, blinking. It was bright in the room. Two gentlemen stood before a small hearth, looking at him. The turnkey let go his collar and said, ' 'Ere 'e is, sirs; this is the brat.' He nudged Joe sharply in the back. 'Bow to the gentlemen, yer young dog!' Joe, confused, bowed, and gazed fearfully at the two men. Was this his trial? It was nothing like he had imagined it would be.

One of the gentlemen stepped forward. 'Where are you from, boy?' he said sharply.

Joe looked up at him. His face seemed kindly, in spite of the sharpness of his tone. 'Please, sir: from near Bradford.'

Croft nodded, suppressing his mounting excitement. 'In which pit do you work?'

'At Rawdon Pit, sir; Mr Rawdon's pit.'

'And what is the name of the gentleman you came to London to see?'

Joe hesitated. Who were these men? Why were they questioning him? The turnkey nudged him again. 'Come: answer the gentleman!' he growled.

' 'Twas Mr Croft, sir. The woman said 'e was in London.'

Croft crouched swiftly, gripping the pale child by both shoulders. 'Listen, child: *I* am Joseph Croft: what message have you for me?' His voice shook.

Joe gasped. '*You*, sir? Oh, don't let 'em 'ang me, sir: I never meant to 'it 'im, nor to steal, sir!'

Croft shook him gently. 'I will see that nothing befalls you; now: what message?'

'Please, sir; it's about t'man in closed road.' Once begun, Joe's words came so fast that Grey, unused to the northern tongue, could barely make out what the child was saying. Nevertheless, what he did hear caused him to gape in disbelief.

''E gave me a button to bring ye, sir, but ye wasn't at 'ome an' they was after us, an' we set out for London but Jimmy was took, an' then I was took an' I 'it 'im an' they caught me an' took the button away.'

Croft shook him again, harder. 'What do you mean, "The man in closed road?" '

'There's a man there, sir, chained up,' said Joe. 'I seen 'im twice.'

Croft straightened up, glancing toward the turnkey. 'Where will the button be now?' he snapped.

'In the Governor's office, sir, same as all the prisoners' things.'

'Take me there.'

'But the boy, sir: I'll 'ave to lock 'im up again first.'

Croft clucked impatiently. 'My colleague here will watch him until we return. Hurry, man; this is desperately urgent!'

The turnkey led him through seemingly interminable corridors, up stone stairs and across a filthy courtyard, until at length they reached the Governor's door, and were admitted. Croft explained his quest rapidly, and the Governor fumbled in a drawer, taking out the button. 'Here it is, sir: it was all the prisoner had on him.'

Croft snatched it, examining it closely. His hands

trembled. 'By God!' he breathed. ''Tis his: this answers much!' He leaned across the Governor's desk. 'I have to travel north in haste,' he rapped. 'How might I have the boy released in my custody?'

'That's a complicated procedure,' said the Governor ponderously. 'A lengthy business.'

Croft brought down his fist on the desk. 'It is a most urgent matter: can you not expedite the procedure?'

The Governor shrugged. 'I will try, sir: but it is unusual; most unusual.'

The arrival of the two gentlemen at the prison had been observed by one of two men who lounged near the gates. He watched, frowning, as a door in the gate was opened to admit them. Then he hurried across the road to where his companion was leaning against a wall, pretending to study a broadsheet.

'Bill!' he whispered, nudging the man. 'D'ye see them two that went in just now?'

'No. What of 'em?' growled Bill.

' "What of 'em?" 'e says! One of 'em was Croft, that's what of 'em!'

Bill let his broadsheet flutter to the ground. 'Croft!' he said hoarsely.

'You *sure*?'

'I know Croft when I sees 'im,' said the other testily. 'I *told* ye we'd best watch an' make sure o' the brat.

'What d'ye reckon Croft's 'ere for?' asked Bill, his face pale.

'To spring the brat, that's what. 'Ere: 'ow much money you got?'

Bill fumbled in his pockets, pulling out coins and dumping them in his companion's. cupped hands. 'That's all of it,' he grunted. 'What ye gonna do?' The man counted, clumsily.

'Buy an 'orse,' he said shortly.

'What for?' asked Bill.

'Ride an' tell Mr Rawdon.'

'Didn't know ye could ride.'

'I were a farmer afore a collier: I can ride fine!'

Another thought occurred to the slow-witted Bill. ' 'Ere! You've took my money; ye can't leave me 'ere wi' nowt!'

'Oh, can't I?' said the other. 'An' 'ow's Mr Rawdon to be warned if I don't?'

'I don't care a button for Mr Rawdon!' cried Bill. 'I'm not starvin' 'ere while you go ridin'!' He lunged at his companion, arms flailing. 'Give me my money! Come on: give it back!' The collier easily dodged his attack and, turning on his heels, he made off rapidly along the street. For a while Bill lumbered after the retreating figure, but the distance between them grew, and at last he stopped, sagged against a wall, and buried his face in his big square hands.

Several hours passed before the necessary permissions were received and the two men strode rapidly out of Newgate with Joe between them. Joe was immeasurably thankful for his deliverance and did not properly understand that it might well be only temporary. He trotted along, answering Croft's anxious questions eagerly.

'He was sick, you say, when you saw him?' said Croft.

'Aye, sir: very sick, 'e looked.'

'How long ago was that?'

'Seven days, sir, I think.'

'Then there's no time to be lost. Grey: when will the next coach leave for the north?'

'It leaves at midday.' Grey consulted his watch. 'And it is almost that now; I fear that we shall not catch it.'

'And the next coach after that?'

'Five tomorrow morning.'

Croft snorted impatiently. 'My brother is rotting in

a stinking hole! Grey: lend me a fast horse and I will ride north.'

'Gladly,' said Grey. 'What of the child?'

'Follow by coach tomorrow: I may have need of you.' Grey nodded his agreement. A passing cab was hailed and ordered off at a fast trot to the mews where his horses were stabled.

16

HUGH RAWDON swung out of the saddle and tethered the hack to an elder. Padgett and the old man were waiting by the winding-gear. He strode over to them, swishing his crop, and addressed Padgett. 'Well: is the fool ready to speak?'

'No, sir. 'E looks weak, sir; can't 'ardly lift 'is 'ead.'

Rawdon snorted. 'By God, but he'll speak, or die without tasting another bite; what of the brat?'

Padgett shrugged. 'E don't know owt, sir: Croft's not told 'im owt.'

Rawdon nodded at the winding-gear. 'Stand to the wheel, Padgett: I shall go down myself.' He reached out, hot with anger, hooking the clatch with the head of his crop.

Padgett went to the wheel. The old man was peering towards the road. 'Sir: there's someone comin': I 'ear an 'orse!'

Rawdon whirled, straining his eyes into the twilight. A rider was leaving the road: coming through a gap in the hedge. He gestured to Padgett. 'Leave that: come away until we know who this is!'

The rider pulled up and slid clumsily to the ground, staggering towards them. 'Mr Rawdon, sir,' he gasped. 'I . . . I came as fast as I could, sir!'

Rawdon, peering at the unkempt figure, recognised one of the colliers he had sent to find Trapper Joe. 'What the deuce d'ye mean, you came as quickly as you could?' he sneered. 'The others got back yesterday.' The man nodded. He was almost dead from exhaustion.

'Aye, sir: and *they* said t'brat was took for armed robbery.' A shadow crossed Rawdon's face. He spoke sharply. 'Well: he *is* at Newgate, is he not?' The man leaned wearily against the headgear, arms hanging limply at his sides. He shook his tangled head.

'No, sir: leastwise, I don't reckon 'e is: I saw Croft goin' in there.'

Rawdon paled. He threw down his crop and grabbed the man by the shoulders.

'When? How long ago was this, man?'

''Twere yesterday, sir; early mornin'. Me an' Bill was watchin' at t'prison.'

Rawdon released his grip and paced back and forth, head thrust forward. A fleck of foam showed on his lip. How had Croft learned of the brat's arrest? He stopped before the collier. 'Did he come out with the brat?'

'Didn't wait to see, sir: got an 'orse an' rode fast as I could. 'Ad to pinch another along the way, sir.'

Rawdon shook his head impatiently. 'Never mind

that. Yes; he'll have got the brat out. This is typical of the man.' He looked sharply toward the road.

'He could be right behind you; he may be here at any moment!' Turning to Padgett, he said, 'Get the men together: the ones you can trust. Bring them here with all speed. I want the closed road collapsed; completely sealed. Is that clear?'

'Wi the two of 'em *in* it, sir?'

'Yes. There must be no trace: an accident. A roof-fall. And hurry, man!'

Padgett turned and made off towards the town. Rawdon turned to the messenger. 'You will come with me,' he rapped. 'You have the pistol?'

'Aye, sir,' said the collier, patting his pocket. The old man stood by the winding-gear.

'You wait there to lower Padgett's men when they

arrive,' Rawdon shouted to him. The old man nodded, muttering. Rawdon gestured towards the collier's lathered horse. 'Mount, and follow me!' he cried. 'We shall arrange a hot reception for one Joseph Croft, should he appear before our work is done!'

Padgett beckoned his men into the tavern's chimney-corner and rapped out his instructions. ' 'E wants it caved-in, an' it's got to look like an accident.' His eyes swept across the hard faces before him. 'An' it's to be done quick, or we're *all* done for.' The men moved towards the door, muttering together. It was one thing to take gold pieces in exchange for silence or an occasional service: quite another to set out on murderous work when the gold might well have stopped for ever. But they had known the secret of Rawdon Pit, and had kept quiet about it. They were all guilty with Rawdon, and would go down with him if he fell foul of the law. They clattered along the road towards the pit. And across the fields beside the road a single figure ran crouching; slipping swiftly from shadow to shadow.

The old man looked up sharply as the collier came bounding over the grass towards the headgear. 'Who's this?' he croaked. 'Who are ye?' He peered short-sightedly. 'Oh, it's you, Tom Fawcett.' Fawcett nodded.

'Aye: wind me down, Jacob, it's quick business I'm 'ere to do!' The old man hesitated, frowning.

'You one o' Padgett's lot?'

'Aye,' snapped Fawcett. 'Padgett sent me: t'others'll be along directly.'

'Why don't ye wait for 'em?'

'I told ye: quick business, an' God 'elp ye if Rawdon 'ears ye 'eld it up!'

The old collier shrugged. 'All right: I'll send ye down. Damned if I know what's goin' on.' Fawcett swung out on the clatch-iron and the old man spat into the grass and bent his back to the wheel.

At shaft-bottom he slid off the bar into the water, gripping his lamp. He splashed between empty corves to the road. He crouched quickly into it, going at a lope; breathing heavily. In the side-gate he pushed back the heavy door and plunged on, swinging out into the far road. He paused here, listening. No sound of the clatch yet. He stumbled on.

At closed road he dropped to his knees, thrusting his lamp inside. The light fell on the first prop, warped and splitting. He shuddered. Deliberately, he thought of the brother he had lost: the brother who had set out to warn Mr Croft of the plot he had overheard and had never returned. He gritted his teeth and crawled in. Here and there the roof sagged, so that it was barely high enough to let him pass. 'It won't take Padgett's men long to make this fall,' he thought grimly.

Presently he heard a metallic rattle ahead and a weak voice croaked, 'You are wasting your time: I will tell you nothing.' This was followed by a fit of harsh coughing. The lamplight fell across a figure propped against the glistening black wall. It might have been a scarecrow, except that it moved a little, and coughed drily. The shaggy head was sunk forward upon the chest. The thin neck was half-hidden by matted hair and filthy, grizzled beard. Fevered eyes were turned on him, burning out of great, grey hollows.

'I'm Fawcett,' he said chokingly. 'I'm 'ere to take ye out.'

From beyond the skeleton a voice cried, 'Mr Fawcett: is it you, sir?'

He swung the lamp, so that the light fell on Jimmy. The boy screwed up his eyes, putting his hands before his face. 'Aye,' muttered Fawcett, ' 'Tis I: an' God forgive me for not 'avin' done this long ago.'

'Ye've come to take us out? What of Mr Rawdon?'

Fawcett fumbled at his belt, unslinging a short pick. 'That's the rub,' he growled, bending to the skeleton's leg-iron. ' 'E's on 'is way 'ere now; leastways 'is men are: an' they mean to bury ye.' He pulled on the length of chain. 'Can ye give an 'and wi' this?' Jimmy shook his tangled head.

'No, sir: my chain won't reach: take care, sir; they're fastened to props!'

Fawcett was hacking at the chain close to Croft's ankle. ' 'Ave to chance that,' he grunted. 'Not much time.' A few heavy blows and the chain parted. The sick man remained propped against the wall, unaware of what was happening. Fawcett crawled over the wasted legs and seized Jimmy's chain. ' 'Ere,' he said. ' 'Old it over this lump.' Jimmy bent forward, holding the links so that two of them lay across a flat stone. At Fawcett's first blow, the prop creaked and a shower of small stones poured down from the roof. He paused, looking up. His face glistened redly in the lamplight. His teeth bit into the lower lip.

'Won't stand much more,' he muttered, and swung

again. More small stones. At the third blow a link broke and Jimmy rolled away from the creaking prop.

'Get t'other side of 'im,' hissed Fawcett. 'An' take 'is legs.' Jimmy crawled over, and Fawcett stuck the pick in his belt and slid his hands under Croft's armpits, dragging him away from the wall. ' 'Old 'is legs an' start backin' along,' he said. Jimmy grasped the thin ankles. It was as much as he could do, in his starved state, to support his own weight. He shuffled backwards, pulling the man after him. Croft's back scraped along the floor. He groaned, rocking his head from side to side. Fawcett shuffled forward on his knees, the lamp clamped between his teeth.

They moved painfully along in this fashion to the main road. Here, Fawcett laid the now unconscious Croft beside the rails, rolling his jacket to act as a pillow. He held up his hand for silence. 'I don't 'ear 'em yet,' he whispered. 'Mebbe we'll get out afore they come.'

'What about 'im, sir?' said Jimmy, nodding toward Croft.

'One of us'll 'ave to 'old 'im on t'clatch: come on, now; they'll be 'ere any minute!' They were stooping to lift the skeletal figure when Fawcett stopped abruptly, holding up his hand. A faint rattling, far away. 'They're 'ere!' he cried. 'Old man'll 'ave told 'em I'm down 'ere! Quick! If they come down wi' pistols we're done for!'

They ran, leaving Croft lying in the road. Fawcett led with the lamp. Jimmy ran behind, panting. He did not know how many days had passed since he had eaten. He knew only that if Rawdon's men reached shaft-bottom, he would never see daylight again.

At shaft-bottom they stopped, looking up. The rattling was becoming louder: the clatch was half-way down. A light glimmered far up in the shaft. Fawcett thrust the lamp at Jimmy. ' 'Ere: take this.' He began seizing empty corves, lifting them: throwing them on to a heap directly under the shaft. Jimmy watched, wondering what the big collier meant to do. The clatch was very close. Fawcett turned, sweating. 'Quick: gimme t'lamp!' He snatched it, whirled it over his head, and smashed it on the corves. Burning oil splashed out, running like liquid gold down between the wooden sides of the vehicles. He ripped off his shirt, held it in the flames, then stuffed it into a gap between corves, just above the water-line. Some of the oil was burning on top of the water, and Jimmy stepped back, coughing.

There came a strangled cry from the shaft as thick smoke rolled into the blackness. Frantic cries of 'Stop t'clatch: pit's on fire!' The clatch stopped, then reversed, hauling its choking burden upward. Fawcett turned to Jimmy.

'That'll 'old 'em a while!' he cried. 'But I 'ope Mr Croft isn't long in gettin' 'ere: they'll be down on us when t'wood runs out!' He pointed to the road. 'Stay 'ere: I'm off to stoke up at yon air shaft!' And he grabbed a blazing plank from the fire and plunged into the road.

The air was stifling. Jimmy backed off, choking. He gazed around at the redly-glistening walls; lit now as they had never been. Fear swept through him.

There was gas in pits. Sometimes there was an explosion. Even a spark could start an explosion. The corves were settling: glowing flakes hissed into the blood-red water. Somewhere, at the back of his mind, a small voice was saying, 'Mr Croft's coming: Trapper Joe must 'ave got to London!' but he could not drag his eyes from the inferno, seeming already to hear the dull boom of an explosion.

Fawcett came back. 'That way's blocked an' all: get up there an' keep it fed. Use props. Knock 'em out wi' this.' He thrust the pick at Jimmy. 'An' don't stand right under t'shaft; they shot at me just now!'

In the road, Jimmy turned. 'What if there's an explosion, sir?' he said. 'Or the roof falls?'

Fawcett shrugged. ' 'Ave to chance it: if *they* get down 'ere we're dead for sure. Just keep that fire goin'!' He turned to his own task and Jimmy ran, carrying the pick and a burning stick to light his way.

At the air shaft the brazier was completely buried under a blazing heap of corves and props. A few props lay ready near by. Jimmy leaned weakly against the wall until the blaze began to settle, then piled on the props, keeping clear of the shaft. He could hear shouting from above. He took the pick, knelt in the nearest working, and began to hack at a prop. As it came away a shower of stones fell about his shoulders.

A sound of hoofbeats reached them through the gathering darkness. Rawdon, crouching behind the thick gorse, hissed, 'Cover your face!' The collier pulled up the kerchief until only his eyes were visible. 'Are the pistols cocked?' The man nodded briefly. Rawdon listened, his head on one side. The rider was very near now. He glanced around, satisfying himself that the horses were well concealed, back in the trees. 'Remember: do not shoot unless you must. Make him turn his back, then strike him down and go through his pockets: it must appear to have been a robbery.' The collier nodded again.

The horseman swept into view around the slight curve. Rawdon peered through the twilight. It was Croft. He touched the collier on the shoulder. 'Now!' Croft hauled on the reins as the masked figure sprang into his path.

' 'Old! Get down, or I'll fire!' Two pistols: one levelled at his head. The horse pulled up, rolling its eyes. The pistol never wavered. Croft dismounted, cursing inwardly. The need to be at his destination blotted out any fear that he might have felt. The thief approached, gesturing with his pistol. 'Turn around: come on; face t'other way!' Croft remained facing the man.

'Look here,' he said. 'My ride is urgent: take my purse and my valuables and let me continue.'

'Oh, aye!' the thief sneered. 'An' 'ave ye ride me down: don't ye wish it might 'appen?' He jerked the pistol again. 'Turn around!' Croft knew he had no choice. Biting his lip in suppressed fury, he turned. The collier moved forward swiftly, pistol raised. A sound, along the road. The man glanced towards it. Croft's boot lashed back, striking him on the knee and the man cried out. Croft threw himself against the man shoulder foremost, and they both fell, Croft's hands clawing for the pistols. The labourer whose whistling had distracted the thief now saw the situation and ran forward brandishing a pitchfork.

The thief had one arm free and was thrusting a muzzle into the snarling face above him when a cold tine slid along his cheek and a voice said, 'Drop the pistols, 'ighwayman, or I'll spit ye!' The thin iron was an inch from his eye: one pistol fell into the mud, and Croft took the other from slack fingers and scrambled to his feet.

'I thank you, my friend!' he said.

' 'Twere nowt,' said the labourer. Croft nodded toward the sprawling thief.

'Keep your fork where it is while I take a look at his face.' He bent down and tore away the kerchief. It was now almost dark, but the small blue scars were still visible on the frightened face. 'You're a collier, aren't you?' he snapped.

The man tried to nod, then remembered the fork. 'Aye.'

'Why did you try to rob me?' The man bit his lip, reluctant to speak. Croft knelt, taking the man by the throat. 'Speak!' he gritted. The man remained silent. The labourer raised his eyebrows enquiringly. Croft nodded. The pitchfork was raised and hung quivering above the horrified collier.

'If I nod again,' said Croft quietly, 'spit him!' The collier put up a hand as though to shield his eyes.

'Keep that there,' growled the labourer, 'an' I'll pin it to yer brains!'

'All right.' The collier's voice was flat; defeated. ' 'Twere Mr Rawdon's doin': I'm no thief.'

'Rawdon wanted me robbed: why?' rapped Croft. The man eyed the pitchfork.

'Mek 'im take that thing away.' Croft turned to the farmer.

'Very well: you may put up your fork.' The man stepped back and the collier sat up.

'If I tell ye,' he said hoarsely. 'Ye'll promise that 'e won't get to me, after?'

'I promise only this,' grated Croft. 'That if you *don't* speak, you will die here and now as an armed robber!' The collier pointed into the trees.

' 'E was 'ere: watchin' from over there. 'E didn't want ye robbed. 'E wanted ye stopped, till t'business at pit were done wi'.'

'Business? What business?'

'They're cavin' it in.'

Croft uttered a harsh cry. 'How long have they been at this?'

'Hour: two, mebbe. It'll be done by now.'

The collier's eyes widened as Croft advanced on him and he made to scramble to his feet. He was half-way up when the pistol-butt struck the side of his head and he crumpled soundlessly into the mud. Croft spun to face the labourer.

'Can you ride?'

'Aye, sir.'

Croft nodded towards his exhausted mount, which stood, head drooping, at the roadside. 'Take my horse: fetch the constables to Rawdon Pit. Tell them to hurry!' The farmer mounted, urging the horse into a reluctant gallop. Croft turned toward the distant pit and plunged into the trees.

The prop was too heavy for him. Dragging it on to the blaze, he came too close to the chimney. A sharp crack and a ball kicked up coaldust at his feet. He threw himself back against the wall, gasping. No air: the fire was burning up the air. 'I can't,' he gasped, shaking his head dizzily. 'I can't dig out any more!' Yet he knew that he must: if the fire settled, they would throw down earth upon it and come swarming down with ropes, to kill him. He would be sealed here for ever. For ever. He wiped an aching forearm across his seared brow and staggered along the flickering red tunnel. On raw knees he crawled into a working. Water fell in a thin stream on to his neck and he paused, turning his roasted face to the cold trickle. He had had the props from here: he must go further in. He moved on until his groping hand found a prop. He swung the pick in a short, weary arc at the place where prop and roof met. The prop moved. He swung again. It fell, clattering hollowly. He was reaching for it when there came a grinding rumble above. Water fell about his head. He screamed, pulling back. The working was filling up; water swirled to his chest, roaring. He backed along the narrow working, keeping his head up. The walls seemed to be disintegrating around him. He came out into the road; staggered upright and backed away, gazing in horror at the water spurting from the mouth of the doomed working. Flying droplets caught the fireglow so that the water flew in a sparkling red arc across the road, shattered on the opposite wall and slid like blood into the scarlet pool that swirled about his feet. He glanced toward the fire. The water was all around the brazier.

Steam rolled up into the smoke. Flecks of burning debris spun on the scummy red surface. The level was rising. Jimmy backed along the road, away from the chimney. Shouts from above. 'Surely,' he sobbed, 'they won't come down now?' The road sloped gently upward here, yet the water was rising around his legs. Croft! Lying helpless just a little way along the road! Jimmy turned from the dying fire, stumbling blindly up the road. He found Croft floundering weakly in the icy blackness. Bending swiftly, he pulled the scarecrow erect, dragging it desperately down towards the side-gate. The water was over his knees now. In his starved condition, even Croft's weight was too much. Just within the side-gate he stopped, falling against the wall; it was black here: the last of the dying fire failed to penetrate. He held Croft under the armpits, keeping the lolling head above water. He was finished: he could go no further. The pit echoed the sounds of its own death. Rushing water and the thunder of collapsing galleries.

A voice, calling to him. He called back, 'Here: I can't move!'

Fawcett, wading along the side-gate, a burning splinter in his hand. 'The water: where's it comin' from?' he gasped. He thrust the torch at Jimmy and took Croft's weight.

Jimmy pointed back along the side-gate. 'A workin' caved in,' he said. 'An' water's pourin' out.'

For the first time, despair showed in the big collier's face. 'Now all they 'ave to do is sit where they are an' keep us down 'ere, an' it'll be all over in an hour!' He glanced down at the water. 'Come on: 'elp me to get 'im to shaft-bottom.'

Jimmy could see no point in reaching shaft-bottom now. His mind was numb with fear. He obeyed Fawcett, mechanically, and they waded on through the side-gate and down the main road.

The water grew deeper as they descended the gentle slope. At shaft-bottom, the last of the fire was crumbling into the water, which now came to Jimmy's waist. There was no smoke, but the men waiting above must have known what was happening, because they were making no attempt to come down on the clatch. They would sit, Fawcett knew, keeping their vigil until the pit was completely flooded: then go away to report the accident. Jimmy looked up the shaft.

'The water'll lift us into the shaft, won't it?' he whispered, seeking a hope to cling to. Fawcett nodded grimly.

'Aye: *us*, not 'im.' He indicated the slumped figure he was holding. 'An' when it does, they'll shoot us like fishes in a barrel.' He nodded to the torch in the boy's hand. 'Keep that 'igh an' dry: there's nowt else, now.'

The fire was gone. They stood, listening to the water: feeling it creep coldly up their bodies. Jimmy sobbed quietly, the torch trembling in his hand. There was no more hope. When Mr Croft came, he would find only a flooded pit. Rawdon would deny that any prisoners had ever existed and nobody would ever be able to prove otherwise.

Both heads jerked erect at the sound of a shot. No ball struck the shaft-side, nor splashed into the water. Another shot and a cry.

'Summat's 'appenin' up there!' cried Fawcett. 'By God, lad, but we might pull through yet!' There were more shots, and some shouting. Jimmy gazed longingly upwards, praying silently that whoever was coming might be in time. The water was still rising. The shouting stopped. The cries died away. They stood chilled and trembling; straining for any sound.

They heard it in the same instant: turned joyful eyes upon each other; gasped, only half-believing. 'The clatch is coming down!' They gazed up into the shaft, which echoed now with the rattle of the chain. Jimmy held up the torch till the swinging bar fell into its flickering light. Fawcett seized it.

A voice called from above, distorted with echo. 'We see your light: call out when we're to raise the clatch!'

Fawcett nodded to Jimmy. 'Get on, young 'un: I'll put this 'un on top of ye.' Jimmy shook his head.

'No: I couldn't 'old 'im: I'm scared on t'clatch, sir, an' need both 'ands to 'old on. You take 'im up an' send it back for me.'

'I'm loath to leave ye 'ere!' cried Fawcett. 'Water's nigh up to yer shoulders!'

'I'm all right, sir: it'll be only for a minute, an' I've got the torch.'

The big collier shrugged. There was a lump in his throat. 'I'll come back for ye,' he said gruffly. He sat on the bar, holding on with one hand, and steadying Croft across his knees with the other. He turned his face upward. 'Haul away!' he yelled. The clatch trembled and rose slowly, lifting Fawcett's feet clear of the water. He looked down at the pale, small boy who stood in the black water, holding high the thin guttering light and gazing upwards. The small face became a smudge and then vanished, and only the twinkling point of light remained to show where he stood.

The disc of stars grew bigger and the clatch bore its burden up into the cold night. Fawcett looked around. It seemed that the whole town was gathered round the headgear. A ragged cheer went up as he appeared. Willing hands pulled in the clatch and he stepped on to the turf. His unconscious burden was taken from him and gently laid in the grass. Joseph Croft knelt beside his stricken brother, cradling the shaggy head in his lap. He looked up as a shadow fell across him. Fawcett, his head silhouetted by the moon. 'My friend,' said Croft. 'You saved my brother's life, and almost lost your own!'

'There's a boy down there, sir!' cried Fawcett. ' 'Ave me lowered again!' Croft came to his feet. He called to some of those who stood watching.

'Lower the collier: there's a lad down there yet!' Fawcett strode to the headgear. Leaning to catch the harness, he felt the rumbling through his feet before his ears registered the sound. Its volume rapidly grew until the ground quaked with the hollow roar of it. The watchers fell back, crying out, as a ball of smoke rolled from the shaft, shot on its underside with dull flickering orange. Fawcett, a cry on his lips, reeled away. The trembling grew. The rim of the shaft was crumbling. Great cracks appeared in the earth around, radiating outward from the gaping roaring hole. Huge chunks of soil and stones tipped, hung poised, then plunged into the shaft. The headgear lurched, its tortured iron screaming as it buckled, tore apart, and toppled out of sight. Now the rumbling seemed to move; echoing away beneath the moonlit fields like thunder in the hills, as distant galleries collapsed. It fell to a far-away echo, so that it became possible to hear the wind in the grass. There were no voices. The people watched the column of smoke that rolled out of the earth. Croft, on his knees beside his brother, heard the ambulance on the distant road, and looked briefly towards the sound. Fawcett, shoulders drooping, stood a little apart. The tears that came to scald pale runnels down his black cheeks might have shamed him, if there had been anyone to see them. The wind moaned over the spoil heaps, and the smoke slanted upward into the stars.

17

THE SPRING SNOW was gone. The earth around the pit was green: ferns uncurled among the crumbling brickwork. Nobody went there now. Figures moved on a distant hillside and the ring of axes sounded on the warm air.

Along the muddy road which threaded the valley midway between the pit and the hill came a pony trap. It drew up and a gentleman got down, turning to help down the small boy who was with him. They moved to the hedge and stood watching the tree-felling along the slope. The gentleman pointed. 'There, Joe: all along there, below where the trees begin. That is where we shall build. A south slope, Joe: the best of the sun, all the year round. And acres of woodland behind to play in when lessons are over for the day!'

Joe looked up at him. 'The woodland's Rawdon's, isn't it, sir?' Croft laughed briefly.

'Rawdon has all the woodlands he needs, I fancy, in New South Wales: and if he ever comes back to England, it won't be to these parts!' Joe frowned.

'Please sir: where *was* the gold, all the time?' Croft smiled.

'You were once very close to it, you and Jimmy,' he said. 'It was in the old mine you hid in when Padgett was after you.' Joe turned away from the hillside, his face taking on an expression of sorrow. Even now, the mention of Jimmy's name caused him sadness. He gazed across to where the old pit lay.

After a moment he said: ' 'E 'ated the dark, sir. An' now 'e's down there for ever.'

Croft laid a hand on the bony shoulder. 'He's not down there, Joe,' he said softly. 'Not the part of him that matters.'

He turned the boy, gently, away from the pit and towards the hillside. 'It is difficult, now, for you to understand, Joe: But some day, you will know.' His voice became very low, as though he were talking to himself. 'Jimmy Booth died in the dark. But a light was kindled here that night: a light that will spread and grow until it lights up every dark place, and by its glow we will see clearly the way to go.' He paused, turning slowly back towards the pit. 'And when that day comes,' he whispered, 'then those of us who knew you will remember: it was lighted from your candle, Trammer Booth.'

These are other Knight Books

Willard Price adventure stories about Hal and Roger and their amazing adventures in search of wild animals for the world's zoos.

1. AMAZON ADVENTURE
2. SOUTH SEA ADVENTURE
3. UNDERWATER ADVENTURE
4. VOLCANO ADVENTURE
5. WHALE ADVENTURE
6. AFRICAN ADVENTURE
7. ELEPHANT ADVENTURE
8. SAFARI ADVENTURE
9. LION ADVENTURE
10. GORILLA ADVENTURE
11. DIVING ADVENTURE
12. CANNIBAL ADVENTURE
13. TIGER ADVENTURE
14. ARCTIC ADVENTURE

These are other Knight Books

These are the adventures of the famous Black Stallion and his friend Alec that are available in Knight

Walter Farley
The Black Stallion
The Black Stallion Revolts
The Black Stallion Returns
The Black Stallion and Satan
Son of the Black Stallion
Black Stallion's Courage
The Black Stallion's Filly
The Black Stallion Mystery
The Black Stallion and Flame
The Black Stallion's Ghost
The Black Stallion and the Stranger
The Black Stallion Legend
The Young Black Stallion

Another Knight Book

BLACK BEAUTY

Anna Sewell

'I was beginning to grow handsome; my coat had grown fine and soft, and was bright black. I had one white foot, and a pretty white star on my forehead.'

Follow Black Beauty's adventures from his first days at his mother's side, onto his life as a working horse and finally to his retirement.

The classic and moving tale of the world's most famous horse.

Jean Webster

DADDY-LONG-LEGS

The story of Judy and her mysterious guardian is one of the most popular romances ever written, and it has been both filmed and made into a highly successful musical.
Judy at seventeen is taken from an Institution, where she is the oldest orphan, and sent to college – at the expense of an amused and anonymous Trustee. A wavering, elongated shadow, once seen, is her only clue, and this induces her to call him Daddy-Long-Legs.

Another Knight Book

Allan Rune Pettersson

FRANKENSTEIN'S AUNT

'Next stop Frankenstein!' Aunt Frankenstein has arrived determined to restore her nephew's devastated castle to order and clear the family's blackened name! An hilariously spooky sequel to the famous Frankenstein story.